A Mind Too Full

BJ Washington

A Mind Too Full
Copyright © 2023 by BJ Washington

All rights reserved. No part of this publication may be reproduced, distributed, or transmitted in any form or by any means, including photocopying, recording, or other electronic or mechanical methods, without the prior written permission of the publisher or author, except in the case of brief quotations embodied in critical reviews and certain other noncommercial uses permitted by copyright law.

Although every precaution has been taken to verify the accuracy of the information contained herein, the author and publisher assume no responsibility for any errors or omissions. No liability is assumed for damages that may result from the use of information contained within.

Library of Congress Control Number: 2023906800
ISBN-13:   Paperback: 978-1-64749-881-8
           ePub: 978-1-64749-882-5

Printed in the United States of America

GoToPublish LLC
1-888-337-1724
www.gotopublish.com
info@gotopublish.com

DEDICATIONS

In Loving Memory of Robert, Ernestine, Mary and Pat.

To Family and Friends, I am sending much love, praying that God will continue and keep you all safe .

A special Thank you to my sister friend Gwen, for her inspiration and continued support.

Will walked over to his window, the window of the small but quaint home that he shared with his wife DeeDee and their seven-year-old son Trey. Will looked out over the beautiful trees, reminiscing on the times before their son was born. They had a lot of time for each other, however not so much anymore. A lot of things went through his mind. He was thinking, and daydreaming about his young son, will our child ever get better? He thought aloud. Will often wondered about his son's health. As a small boy, only two years old Trey was experiencing uncontrollable outburst out of nowhere. The outburst turned from rage, fits of anger, sometimes to the point of self-destruction.

Will Wilson and DeeDee have been married for 11 years. Will was an electrician by trade, DeeDee was a fifth-grade schoolteacher. She took a leave of absence; DeeDee was now a stay-at-home mom. Even though they lived off one income, the two made it work.

A scream jolted him back to earth with a stark, his wife was yelling from Trey's bedroom upstairs. "Will come, come quickly!" Will ran for the stairs, entering Trey's bedroom Will saw his son banging his head against this wall. He ran over to his son, grabbed him and pinned him down on the bed. Trey struggled to break free, but undoubtedly his father was much stronger than him. Trey continued to struggle until his mother came over to him and whispered in his ear, "It is okay baby momma is here, momma is here." DeeDee began to whisper in her son's ear. Trey finally started to relax. Will could feel the tension ease against his body, he slowly released his grip. The look on Trey's face was that of a cute little cherub. He sat on the side of his bed looking around as if he were trying to figure out where he was. He looked at his mom, "What is all that red stuff on the wall?" he asked. Trey had drawn blood. "My head hurts," he said. DeeDee led her son to the bathroom where she cleaned him up and took care of his bruises. Will cleaned the blood from the wall. It is a good thing that Will was home because he would have overpowered his mother. Trey was big for a seven-year-old.

Trey had been to several doctors over the years. But none of them found anything neurologically wrong. His pediatrician, Dr. Anderson attributed his behavior to that of childish tantrums that he would grow out of.

DeeDee was filled with faith, DeeDee was a praying woman. She believed that the miracle of God would get her family through anything. DeeDee was right!

Will and DeeDee had decided that it would be best to hire a Home Care Nurse, Trey was getting taller and stronger. His outbursts were becoming more frequent. DeeDee could use the extra hands during the day. DeeDee had called the referral agency to have them send potential candidates to her so that she and her husband could decide who to hire. They would sit down after dinner when Trey was asleep and go over the resumes.

There was one that stood out above all the others, that one was Nurse Rita Collins. The Wilsons would find out later down the line that Rita Collins was not her real name, and she was not the person on her resume. DeeDee would call and schedule her for an interview. Will and DeeDee retired for the evening, settling on Nurse Rita Collins to come tomorrow after Trey's lunch break.

DeeDee was the first to rise, she was already in the kitchen preparing breakfast. Will came down to the kitchen ready for his breakfast. He told his wife that he might have to work a little longer, but he would be home directly after. Ok she said and reminded him of the interview from the agency. Will would not be able to attend after all. Trey entered the kitchen just before his father left for work. Trey gave his father a big hug, Will tussled his son's hair and gave him a kiss on his forehead, "do not give your mother a hard time today," Will left. Trey appeared puzzled. "I never give my mommy a hard time," he thought to himself. That's because he pretended not to remember his actions during and after his explosions.

The two had breakfast, cleared the table and cleaned the dishes. Trey always helped his mother. They went into the office where his desk was set up. The morning session started at eight thirty am. Then there was lunch break, before the afternoon session. The same routine day in and day out. Today was the exception. DeeDee was to interview the new nurse. I will ask her to join us for lunch, DeeDee thought to herself. If everything worked out. DeeDee thought that she may be able to return to teaching part time.

It was ten till twelve, the doorbell rang. Trey grabbed onto his mother's skirt and held on tight. She went to the door with her son in tow. Dragging him because he wouldn't let go of her skirt. When she finally answered the door, he had scooted behind his mother peeking out to see who was at their door.

DeeDee opened the door for Nurse Rita Collins. DeeDee led her into the living room. Trey is still hiding. "Hello," she held out her hand to DeeDee and introduced herself. "I am Rita Collins," "hello I am DeeDee Wilson." "It's a pleasure to meet you, Mrs. Wilson," "pleasure is all mine, and please call me DeeDee." Trey is still behind his mother. He peeked again to see who was talking to his mom. Rita leaned in at Treys eye level, she began to speak. Suddenly, he let out a blood curdling scream, a scream resembling that of a wounded animal. Trey came from behind his mother and lunged at the nurse, kicking her in her shin knocking her to the floor and before DeeDee could stop him he was on the woman pounding her with closed fist, small but powerful. The nurse tried several times to get up, when finally, his mother yelled at him. "Trey stop it! Stop it! What has gotten into you?" DeeDee caught hold of his shirt and pulled him back. Rita got her bearings. But Trey was still trying to get at her. "Rita, please go into the kitchen and get the syringe from the drawer nearest the refrigerator and bring it to me." Rita returned with the syringe in hand and jabbed Trey in his left arm. He was still trying to kick her again. The medication took effect, Trey fell silent in his mother's arms. The two exhausted women carried him over and placed him on the sofa. He was much too heavy to carry to his room. Anyway, DeeDee needed to keep eyes on him.

Rita collected herself and her things and headed for the door. "I am so sorry Rita, he has never acted out on anyone before. I have never seen that side of my son before" DeeDee said to the nurse. "Please except my sincerest apologies." Rita grabbed DeeDee's hand and said "it's ok Mrs. Wilson, I mean DeeDee I have been a psychiatric nurse for five years now and believe me I have experienced a lot worse." She told DeeDee that if she still wanted her, she could come back and try again. "Oh, my you are willing to come back, that would be wonderful, I will give you a call later in the week if that's ok." "Yes, that will be fine." DeeDee thanked Nurse Rita Collins as she left. Rita thought to herself. "I will get that little monster in line; I will teach him some respect! He is strong and that kick really hurt."

Nurse Rita Collins had worked at the Psychiatric hospital in Mapleton, Florida for more than five years. She was confident, and very competent. She was not who she was presumed to be. Rita had gone to great lengths to change her identity. She appeared very reputable on paper. Rita was assuming the name of a deceased woman. Yes, that is correct. A dead woman. The person not on the resume was Shelia Monture. She had embezzled, committed wire fraud as well as child abuse. She changed her name when she was twenty, some ten years ago. She had gone under the knife, had plastic surgery on her face. Rita, aka Shelia had gotten away with her new identity. Life had gone well for Rita Collins without a hitch. But would anyone ever find out? Rita never bothered much about that.

Trey started to stir; he woke up but was still a bit groggy. He asked his mother, who was preparing dinner, "Mother why am I on the sofa?" DeeDee did not answer him. Trey knew his father didn't like him sleeping on the sofa for fear that he might wet on it. "Daddy should be here any minute now, go wash up for dinner." By the time Trey returned his dad had come in and was in his chair watching the news channel. "Hi daddy" Trey greeted his dad, "hello son, were you a good boy for your mother today?" "Yes, daddy I am always a good boy." DeeDee looked through to the living room and gave her husband a look of shear disgust. She put her finger to her lips, so as to let Will know to please do not ask right now. He caught on quickly. "Dinner is ready you two."

They all sat down to dinner; it was both their favorites. Fried chicken with mac and cheese. "Yummy!" Trey exclaimed "I just love Mac n Cheese." Will didn't say much, he was still wondering why his wife had given him the silent finger. This must be a doosey he thought. Will put the silent finger in the back of his mind, at least until Trey was out like a light. He told his wife of his day. He also mentioned to her that maybe soon you and I can go on a date. "You know like normal couples." "A date night?" DeeDee snickered like a schoolgirl, if she had been of the lighter complexion Will may have seen her cheeks redden from her blushing. DeeDee was a beautiful woman, dark brown complexion and she had colored her hair a crazy red. Will on the other hand was tall, stout with a light complexion. A handsome fellow. Trey favored his mother more. He had a medium complexion, a blend of his mom and dad. He had curly cold black hair, dimples so deep that he needed not smile for them to be noticed, Trey also had a clef chin, he was a handsome child.

Will and DeeDee tucked their son in bed. The two took their showers and climbed into bed as well. DeeDee began to fill Will in on the events of the day. When she was done, Will sat up in bed slack jawed stunned at what his wife had told him. He could not believe his ears, DeeDee went on to tell him that the nurse wanted to return, "what? She wants to come back!" DeeDee told Will that she really liked the nurse. Will said "yes but you are not the one who will spend most of the time with her." DeeDee agreed. "What shall I do? I guess it would be ok to give it one more try. I pray it works the next time she comes. What did you say Will?" DeeDee asked her husband. He looked perplexed! "You said you pray," "do not get any ideas honey it was just a figure of speech. Good night sweetie. Rest well," she said to her husband. They turned the lights out and slept.

The next morning, the ritual continued. Breakfast, dishes, kisses, goodbyes. Trey was very quiet at the table this morning and also when he helped his mother clean the kitchen. They went into the office as usual. Trey got his first session, then lunch. Nurse Rita came back during lunch. Trey's reaction was no different, for whatever reason or reasons he did not like Rita. This time he landed a really good kick to her shin, Rita's shin was still sore, so it hurt even worse. She did not lose her balance and fall this time, she gathered her belongings and left, not without letting DeeDee know how she felt. "Something is seriously wrong with your son, and if you don't believe it and get him some help then there is something wrong with you too!" Rita slammed the door as she left.

Lunch time arrived. DeeDee placed Trey's lunch in front of him at the table. Trey sat there with his elbows on the table, no, fist clenched, resting on his cheeks, he wasn't saying a word. When he did speak he made a point to let his mother know never to bring that woman back here. "I don't like her!" he banged his fist on the table. He repeated himself. "I do not like her!" He jumped up from his chair, It landed on the floor. He went to his room and slammed the door.

DeeDee did not bother him. She didn't even finish the afternoon session.

When Will came to the phone, she was crying. "Come home now, Will! Now!"

DeeDee slammed the phone down. She locked herself in her room until she heard Will come up the steps. When Will entered the bedroom, DeeDee was on her knees in prayer. Will turned to go down the hall to Treys room.

He opened the door and Trey hit his father hard over the head with a chair. Will, still trying to recuperate from being blind-sided, was hit again.

He called out to his son, "Trey, stop it! Please, son, stop it!"

Trey paused, "I told her I didn't like that lady."

No, he had not told his mother that or she would never have allowed her back, Will thought.

"Okay son, she is gone, and she will not be coming back," Will said, pacifying his son. Trey laid down on his bed and fell asleep.

DeeDee was still reeling from the incidents that had occurred. Will sat on the side of the bed,

"That boy needs to be put away," he told his wife. DeeDee would not hear of that.

No, she said emphatically. No, our son will not be placed away behind bars like some animal.

"There must be another way," she cried. Will held his wife and stroked her back to try and comfort her as best he could.

Will slept with one eye open. They never awakened Trey, just let him sleep through the night. While Trey was out cold Will and DeeDee changed him into his pajamas.

Will arose at 4:15 a.m. and went in to check on his son. He had destroyed his room. Trey broke past his father and tore running frantically through the house, screaming, taking down anything in his path. Will, right behind him, caught his son, restrained him; and threw him to the floor. DeeDee had his medication ready. She jabbed him with the needle and Trey went limp "Where in the name of fried chicken did that come from?" Will asked his wife. "Honey, I don't know, but he hasn't been the same since that nurse was here. We cannot continue to live like this. You are the one who spends most of the time with him and you are scared to death to be alone with him. We don't know when he will act out. There must be a better way."

Will and DeeDee sat holding each other. Will was still beside himself; they wouldn't let Trey out of their sights. Trey was acting as if it was just a normal night. Him being his happy-go-lucky self. He appeared to be normal except for when he was manic. Lately, his outbursts had become more frequent.

Will carried Trey to his room. Another night without sleep, he thought. They went to bed; however, neither of them slept much. It was three am. When Will went to check on Trey on his room, Trey was gone. He searched the house, no Trey. It was as if he had vanished.

Will went to his bedroom; got his wife out of bed.

"Trey is gone. I have looked everywhere, he's not here, honey. Trey is not here!"

"Call the police!" DeeDee said. Will went to grab his cell phone and dialed 911.

"My boy is missing," Will told the officer who answered. He was in a panic.

"Calm down," the officer instructed him. "Slowly tell me what is going on." Will followed and relayed all information until the call ended.

"There will be someone here soon," Will told DeeDee. They both sat on the couch and waited. Several minutes later, the doorbell rang. Will hurried to the front door, and yanked it open to let the officers in. One of them introduced himself as Officer Todd.

Will frantically relayed the events of the last evening and the morning again before the call.

"Does your son have any friends or family in that he would go to?" Officer Todd asked.

"No, no. It's just us on this side of town. He has an aunt, my wife's sister, but we called, and she hasn't seen or heard from Trey. His name is Trey, Trey Allan Wilson. He's about five feet tall. He is African American and, my god, he's only seven years old."

"Do you have a picture of Trey, Mr. Wilson? And what was he wearing when you saw him last?" one officer asked them.

"Yes, I will get a picture," DeeDee told the officer.

"He was wearing Superman pajamas last I saw him. But his pajamas were on his bedroom floor when I checked his room. I can't say what he changed into," Will recalled.

"We will put out an amber alert, as well as an All-points bulletin. Please try and remain calm. We will do our best to locate your boy," Officer Todd told them. "We will be in touch." Officer Todd handed Will his card and both officers left. Shortly after, Liz, DeeDee's sister arrived. Liz came into the house, gave everyone a hug, and sat with them in the kitchen. While DeeDee was making coffee, Will called his boss, Benny. He relayed the issues and told him to put him on Family Medical leave for a few days. Hopefully, Trey will have been found by then. Benny told Will to take all the time he needed.

"Please keep me informed," Benny said to Will before they ended their conversation.

"I have said more than several times, he needs to be in a hospital. He's not well, hasn't been for years now." The previous day, Trey had destroyed dinner. DeeDee was done cooking, so he decided to throw a fit. He went into the kitchen, removed every pot from the stove, took the lids off, and emptied all the food in the sink. His mother stood and watched, afraid that if she tried to stop him, or intervene in any way, for fear Trey might hurt her. Will arrived home that day and dinner had been ruined. He went in to scold his son and, of course, he did not have a clue as to what his father was talking about. They ordered dinner from take out. There were so many episodes, they stopped counting. "Okay, now, when he's found, what do we do?" Will asked the two ladies sitting across from him.

"We bring him back home," DeeDee said to her husband. "We continue to care for him as best we can, just as we have always done."

"But this time is different," Liz chimed in. "This time, he has taken off to only God-knows-where. A seven-year-old boy in the wicked streets alone."

"He can't be far," Will scarfed at Liz. Will just shook his head and DeeDee was in her state of depression again.

Lord, please help us, she prayed. *Are we to put our son away?* DeeDee asked God.

Liz stayed overnight to be on hand if Trey returned home. Or if Will and DeeDee needed her. She always slept on the sofa even if there was an extra bedroom. Liz preferred to be near the door. Liz slept on the first floor near the door of her home too. There was something about Liz being able to get out quickly if she needed to.

No one was able to get much sleep. It was 7 a.m. and still no word concerning Trey. DeeDee was worried sick. *My poor baby boy, out there all alone, she repeated that train of thought. He was never alone because Jesus was always with him. He would hear that from his mother whenever he was afraid. Always pray and ask for guidance, she told him. Trey would always ask, but why can't I see him, mommy?* She would only reply, *Oh, but he can see you, my sweet boy, and that's all that matters.*

There was a gas station about a mile away from the Wilson home. The attendant ran the station on the night shift. It was nearing 7:30 a.m., almost time for his shift to end. He went to take a leak before driving for an hour to his home. The attendant went outside to the restroom, but it was locked. He could clearly hear a child sobbing.

"Hello?" he called at the door. There was no answer, just a child sobbing. He went back inside, called the police and explained the situation. A few minutes later, two patrol cars pulled into the station, sirens blaring lights flashing. The attendant approached the officers, then led them around the side to the restroom. The one officer knocked on the door, he heard the boy crying also.

"Do you have a key?" the officer asked the attendant.

"Yes, I do but I was afraid to open it for fear of what I might find," The attendant opened the door and there sat a child huddled in the corner, dirty and wet. He had soiled his pants. The officer slowly approached the child. "What is your name, son?" Trey didn't answer, the officer knew who he was because he had a picture of him. It was all over the radio that this seven-year-old boy was missing.

Trey slid from out of the corner and began to move toward the officers. They asked him again what his name was.

Trey responded. "My name is Trey Allan Wilson," Trey always gave his full name when asked.

"Okay then, Trey Allan Wilson, we are going to get you back to your parents. Is that okay with you son? asked the nice policeman.

Trey shook his head and then said yes, remembering not to shake his head. His mother had taught him that it was rude to shake your head. The other officer had gone to the trunk of the police cruiser to retrieve a blanket that was kept there for emergencies. He placed the blanket around Trey and led him to the patrol car. Trey rested his head against the back seat and let out a sigh of relief.

When they pulled into the police station, a female officer came out to the car. The officer had radioed the station to let everyone know that the missing child had been found. The female officer took Trey to one of the interview rooms. She asked Trey if he wanted something to eat or drink. He responded, "No, thank you."

The detective assigned to the case from the missing and abused children's unit called the Wilsons. He explained that their son appeared to be alright. And that they should come down to the station with a fresh set of clothes because Trey had soiled himself.

Child protective services had been called as well. How and why was this child found in a seedy gas station restroom, soiled. Where had his parents been? Those were the questions that needed to be answered. Detective Robinson and Detective Nells, along with Ms. Singleton from CPS, were in the interview room, all waiting for Will, DeeDee, and Liz to arrive.

The clerk at the front desk pointed to interview room number four. DeeDee was so excited, she was running and almost fell. Will gave a tap on the door; Detective Robinson opened the door and invited them in. DeeDee ran over to her son, all the while Will was standing like a bump on a log, showing no emotion. Trey did not respond to his mother; however, she was allowed along with a female officer to take Trey to the restroom to get changed.

It was strange that Trey did not respond to his mother nor his father. This was another question the CPS lady would ask. My work is always such a challenge, thought Ms. Singleton. DeeDee returned to the interview room with Trey.

"Your son will need to be taken to the hospital to be checked out." This came from Detective Robinson who was the lead on Trey's case.

"Yes," said DeeDee. "My husband and I will take him."

"No, Mrs. Wilson. I am afraid that's not how it works, because of the circumstances of the situation, this is now a case for the police and child protective services. Your son, being a minor and all, there must be an investigation. You are welcome to meet us there if you like."

"If we like, you say that, detective, as if we don't care about our child and that we have done something to feel guilty about." Dee Dee retorted. Will didn't say a word, which further drew suspicions to the couple.

Liz was waiting outside. She knew nothing of what had taken place in the interview room. DeeDee told Detective Robinson that they would meet them at the hospital. DeeDee stormed off in a huff. Trey was put into Ms. Singleton's car and driven off toward Lake Street where the hospital was located. Will still had not spoken a word. There wasn't a peep from DeeDee's husband and their son's father.

They arrived at the hospital at about the same time. DeeDee walked past the CPS lady and didn't say anything. However, she had an awful lot to say, just not right now. She had to get her son home safely before she could let the fireworks off.

Trey was taken into examination room number four, the same number as the interview room at the precinct. She thought it coincidental. There were two doctors and a nurse in with Trey, along with Detective Robinson. And accompanying Ms. Singleton was the doctor on staff and the other was a psychiatrist.

"When can we take our boy home?" Will finally spoke. DeeDee glanced over at her husband, but she didn't utter a word. She had a few things to discuss with him at home.

"We would like to keep him overnight for observation," the psychiatrist answered.

"That will be fine, doctor. I will get started on my investigation," Ms. Singleton was the next to speak. "I will let you know of my findings." Then she left without addressing the Wilsons other than to say, "I will be in touch." They all gave Trey hugs and kisses, then left. But it did hit the fan when DeeDee got her husband home. No one said a word on the ride back to the house. Liz decided that she would get in her car and head back to her home, because she want to hear any part of the screaming Will was going to receive from his wife. Liz did not understand how so much had gone wrong in the last seventy-two hours, but all her sister wanted to do was fuss and Will didn't have anything at all to say. Liz thought, What is going on with those two? What in the world was happening with my nephew?

DeeDee walked in the house first. Will dragging in behind her like a dog with his tail between his legs. He knew he was about to feel her wrath. She prayed a lot, but she also would not hesitate to say what was on her mind when it was necessary.

"Before you say anything," Will said to his wife, "I am really relieved that Trey is not here tonight. I need some sleep and a piece of mind." "What?" She let go of her husband.

"You have been distant from our son for some time now. You go to work, come home, never taking time with him. You continually bicker with me about putting him away. The show you put on about him being missing was just that from what I saw. You never once comforted him in the hospital. I know you love him, but you have a very strange way of showing it."

"I want him to be well, I want him to be a normal boy. Not some lunatic," Will said this with tears in his eyes. "I want what we used to have. I want my wife back!"

"Well, you can't have your wife without your son, William Wilson. And don't you ever form your mouth to call my son a lunatic! Not ever, do you hear me?" DeeDee yelled to the top of her voice and left Will sitting on the sofa to feel sorry for himself. Not for his child but for himself. Shame on him.

Will and DeeDee stayed away from each other for the rest of the evening. DeeDee sobbed uncontrollably, she wanted her son home and safe with her. Her faith would not allow her to give up or give into her husband's wishes to put her boy away.

Trey was as calm as if nothing had happened to him. His father thought it was an act, he thought Trey knew exactly what he was doing. He felt that he could fool his mother, but he wasn't fooling his father.

The next morning, the Wilsons had breakfast and then went directly to see their son. DeeDee drove.

Will broke the ice. "I am sorry about yesterday, honey."

"I am sorry too, Will" DeeDee replied to her husband. "Let's put it behind us and start fresh."

"Okay," he reached over and took hold of her hand and kissed it, just like he used to.

They arrived at the hospital, stopped at the reception desk.

"Good morning, we are here to see our son. His name is Trey Wilson."

"Yes, he is on the eighth floor."

"He was in emergency when we left last night."

"They moved him," the clerk responded.

"Oh, alright, thank you," Will said and they headed to the elevators. Once inside and the doors closed, Will pulled his wife tight, kissed her square on her lips. She blushed and kissed him back. The doors opened, they held hands and proceeded to go see Trey.

"Honey," Will stopped his wife in the middle of the corridor before reaching Treys room, he looked her in her eyes and teared up a bit. "You know I didn't mean those things that I said yesterday. I was so frustrated I wasn't thinking."

"I know you love him," DeeDee said. "Let's go see him please."

Trey was in a private room; he had an episode last night, so they moved him to the children's ward. He has been sedated, his nurse told them. Her name was Tina, she introduced herself.

"Hi Tina, I am DeeDee, his mother and this is Will, Trey's father. What happened last night?"

"Well, the ER nurse gave him an IV because he was dehydrated. She put it in his arm, tapped it down, and Trey went into a rage. He started hitting her, pushing her away. He tried several times to get out of bed. Two orderlies came to restrain him, he was much too strong for her to handle alone. During the struggle, his IV came out of his arm. After reinserting it, he was sedated and put in arm restraints.

"The doctors ordered him to be moved to this floor. They will be running a battery of tests. There is something very wrong. But he's in the best place." Tina patted DeeDee on her shoulder, told them to have a nice visit. "He would be going down to begin testing in an hour. You are welcome to stay if you like. "

"I will stay, Will," DeeDee said. "You go back to work. There is no reason for us both to be here right now. He doesn't even know we are here."

"Please keep me posted honey. If you need me, call. I love you!" Will kissed her on her cheek and left.

Trey was a loner; his parents kept him secluded because of his outbursts. He had never known peers, therefore he never missed having them.

There will be a meeting of the minds soon, a meeting that all concerned will be present. The conference room was located on the fifth floor of the hospital. Dr. Fitzgerald was the head of the psychiatry department at Helena Memorial Hospital in Mapleton, Florida.

Trey was still sedated; he had been taken down to the x-ray lab to begin a series of tests. The tests more than will likely take several days. It doesn't look like Trey would be going home anytime soon. His doctors thought it best to start the tests while Trey was still sedated. Especially the tests that require him to remain still.

DeeDee sat in his room for well over an hour, waiting for her son's return. She called Will to update him on the progress. "I will come by after work," he told her.

"Call first," DeeDee said to him, "If he is not awake when they bring him back to his room, I may go home and come back later."

"Oh honey, whatever you think is best."

She waited for another hour; she told the nurse that she would be back later. Maybe he'll be awake by then.

DeeDee went home to the empty house that was a total mess. It had not been tidied from Trey's tantrum three days ago. One thing happened after another. No time to clean. No time to tidy. She decided to put things back in order while she was home alone. She made herself lunch, after which she tackled the task at hand. When DeeDee was finished, she breathed a sigh of relief.

"This is my tidy, little home again," she said out loud. She smiled, an expression that had not been on her face so frequent lately.

The next day, she and Will went to the hospital together. It is conference day. Will would go to work late. He wanted to be in the loop. The conference room was on the first floor. When Will and DeeDee arrived, there were several people there. The one that stood out to her was the woman from Child Protective Services. DeeDee found seats far away from her as possible.

The room was comfortable. Not too hot and too cold, DeeDee didn't like being cold. The doctors sat at the far end of the table. In attendance were Dr. Fitzgerald, the psychiatrist; Dr. Thompson, Trey's pediatrician; Dr. Colder, the head doctor at the hospital; Dr. Teleflora, the head of neurology; the surgeon who would be performing the surgery, Ms. Singleton, the woman from CPS; and Will and DeeDee.

Dr. Colder stood and introduced himself and asked everyone to introduce themselves. When the introductions were now out of the way, Dr. Colder turned the meeting over to the psychiatrist. Dr. Fitzgerald stood at the front of the room with Trey's x-rays from the day before. With a pointer in hand, he led everyone to Trey's brain. Circling a mass of a white substance, he explained that the mass was abnormal. This is likely the cause of Trey's outbursts.

"We will need to go in, operate to remove the mass, have it analyzed before we can say further what it is. It resembles that of a tumor; however, there are some other abnormalities that cannot be seen with the naked eye causing the possibility that it may not be a tumor. At any rate, we won't know anything further until after the surgery."

Ms. Singleton raised her hand and asked if she could speak, because she would be leaving. Yes, they gave her the floor.

"Thank you," she said and went on to say her investigation had been concluded. "There was no evidence of child abuse in my findings. The investigation is now closed. All the best to you, Mr. and Mrs. Wilson."

DeeDee was elated to hear that bit of news. Now, we can concentrate on Trey getting better. However, she was still reeling and shaking at the doctor's report. She looked at her husband, Will.

"Surgery?" Then she addressed the all the doctors. . "Is there no other way, he's only seven."

Dr. Teleflora spoke. "Mrs. Wilson, this surgery is not uncommon. I assure you that I have performed hundreds of brain surgeries in my career. Children are not immune from sickness as you well know. Please take some time to talk it over. The surgery will be scheduled when you both decide. In the meantime, we would like to keep him here at the hospital until you let us know of your decision."

"Yes, there are a lot of questions that must be answered. We will get back to you as soon as possible," Will told the doctors. "Now we would like to visit with our boy."

The two bid a good day to the doctors and left.

The doctors discussed a few things before ending the meeting. Dr. Fitzgerald pulled a file from his briefcase.

"I took the liberty to pull the child's medicals from birth, with the permission of Dr. Thompson. It looks like he has been suffering from mental issues since the age of two. Fits of anger, and uncontrollable rage. He had been seen by two psychiatrists. In my opinion from what I have read, this child should have long since been placed under psychiatric supervision. It reads that he has been prescribed medication and has seen therapists on occasion. However, his bouts have gotten worse over the years."

Dr. Teleflora chimed in. "Let's hope and pray that his parents agree to the surgery. Sooner rather than later. If not, then it will become a court issue. He cannot continue without the surgery. We need to find out what the mass is and if it's causing his mental issues."

Trey was back in his room. He was awake having his lunch with Will and DeeDee sitting with him. Will was about to leave to return to work. The little boy in front of him was the son he knew when he was in his right mind. Will had refused to admit that his son had a mental problem. He guessed mainly due to his doctors recognizing it as only childish tantrums. Will kissed Trey on his forehead, tussled his afro, and said, "See you soon, be kind to your nurses, and don't give your mother a hard time either."

DeeDee told her husband goodbye, and she would let him know if she could stay with Trey for the night. DeeDee decided that she would go home and talk with her husband concerning the possible upcoming surgery on Trey. She sat with him a little longer but would leave soon enough to prepare dinner for Will. Trey was where he needed to be. He would be watched 24/7. She and Will would finally get some time alone and a good night's sleep. She kissed him on his cheek, told him that she would see him tomorrow. He didn't fret, he said, "*Okay mommy, bye, bye.*" DeeDee left.

DeeDee stopped at the market on her way home. Such a relief to leave Trey and know that he was safe. She bought the necessary items and headed home.

When Will arrived home at five forty-five on the dot, she had prepared a wonderful dinner. The house smelled good. The aroma from the kitchen reminded Will of old times. Oh, they had eaten together every evening, but it was mostly on pins and needles. They never knew when Trey would act out.

Will always believed that Trey was aware of his actions, but after seeing his x-rays, not so much anymore. He had reservations concerning mental illness. He wanted his son to be well. He and his wife would have uninterrupted time this evening to discuss the matters at hand. He was looking forward to a peaceful night at home alone with his wife. He almost felt like praying. He didn't get on his knees, that was too much. But he did thank God for his blessings. Something Will rarely had done.

Will kissed DeeDee on her cheek. "It smells great in here," Will took special notice to how nicely his wife had dressed for their dinner and some much-needed alone time. She looked and smelled as good as his dinner.

"You look beautiful," he said to her, and he went over and embraced her. No looking over his shoulder to see if the little guy was coming into interrupt.

Will washed up, he didn't even go to the living room to his chair. He set the table for DeeDee. That had been Trey's job. After setting the table, Will sat and waited for dinner to be served. DeeDee would always have dinner ready by six. They started to chat about Trey's surgery. She placed dinner on the table. They could even have a glass of wine. Dinner is served, she said. DeeDee blessed the food, and they ate and talked. The two sat in conversation long after they finished the feast, sipping wine and enjoying each other's company. It's been so long since there and only been the two of them.

It was nine p.m. They realized how long they had been sharing each other's company.

"Oh, honey look what time it is," DeeDee said.

Will responded with an old cliché. "Time flies when you're having fun."

They both laughed. Will rose from the table to help DeeDee with clearing and cleaning the dishes. That had also been Trey's job.

The dishes had been washed, dried, and put away. DeeDee's kitchen was nice. Clean and neat, just the way she liked. The two had come to an agreement concerning Trey's surgery. They thought it was the best for all of them. They would let the doctors know in the morning.

Mr. and Mrs. Wilson retired to their bedrooms for the night. "Lights out," Will said with a sinister laugh.

DeeDee knew what exactly that meant. Afterwards they cuddled and slept like babies all night long.

Morning came much too soon; they were still in each other's arms when the dreaded alarm went off. It was six a.m. and the time for Will to get ready for work. DeeDee would make breakfast, then head to the hospital. Will told her that he would go with her, but she said that she would be fine.

"I can handle things; you can come after work."

"Alright then, I will see the two of you later. Call me if you need me."

DeeDee had a full understanding of what questions to ask Trey's doctors.

Trey was sitting up in bed.

"Hello, mommy," Trey held out his arms for his mother's embrace.

"Hi, honey," she went over and gave him a big fat kiss on his cheek. "How did you sleep last night?," she asked as she took a chair beside his bed.

"I don't remember what,"he told her. "I really don't remember, mommy." The tone in Trey's voice changed. DeeDee did a double take.

"Okay, baby, it's alright if you don't remember. You will get better soon," she reassured her little one.

The doctor on duty was making his rounds, and he came to say hello to DeeDee and Trey. He told DeeDee that his vitals were good and that he had slept well.

"Hospitals don't let you get much rest." They laughed. "He also hasn't had any more outbursts since he woke from the sedation."

DeeDee mentioned to the doctor that Trey said he didn't remember if he slept.

"That's normal for the diagnosis that was given," the doctor reassured. "Did you and your husband decide on him having the operation?"

"Yes, we did and yes, we are."

"That's wonderful. His doctors will be in to discuss the particulars sometime today."

"Yes, I have some questions for them, if they are not answered after we meet."

The doctor bid her a good day, waved goodbye to Trey, and left. Trey's breakfast had arrived. It was oatmeal, toast, one egg scrambled with milk, and orange juice. Treys sat up and said, "Yummy, yummy mommy. Just like home."

Not like home, DeeDee thought to herself. He never eats oatmeal, and he hates eggs He ate every morsel of the hospital food. What the, she almost said out loud. She caught herself.

Will called to check on his family, Liz also called. Liz was coming to visit later in the day. Will will be coming to see Trey on his lunch break, because he may need to work late, pick up some overtime. It surely couldn't hurt. Although he had checked with HR at work and there was more than enough insurance to cover medical expenses. Maybe he would take the extra monies and buy his wife something nice.

Trey's doctors arrived in full force. There were six people in white jackets who entered the room. Dr. Teleflora, the neurosurgeon, came over to shake DeeDee's hand and relay to her who was present. She knew three of the doctors from the conference. Dr. Teleflora told her one was a resident and the other doctor was an intern. "Have you and Mr. Wilson opted to let Trey have the surgery?"

"Yes, we have decided to go forward, but first I have some questions."

"Shoot," the doctor said.

"Well first on a scale of one to ten, what are the risks? Two, how long will the surgery last? And three, what are his chances of a full recovery?"

"Those are great questions." The doctor answered all her questions and then some. She was satisfied and felt confident that, along with prayer, their son would be fine. The doctors said they would be in touch and left.

Trey was still sitting as docile as a lamb, and coloring in the coloring book the nurse had given him. He didn't say a word after his breakfast. It was now almost lunch time.

"Will and Liz should be here soon," DeeDee uttered this out loud, but she was just talking to herself. No response from the child sitting in the bed right beside her.

She let his nurse know that she was going to the cafeteria. "I will be right back, Trey," she told him. He never looked up from his coloring book.

When she returned, Will was in the chair, and Liz was there also. She was happy to see them both. Hugs and kisses were exchanged, but still no response from Trey Allan Wilson. It was if they weren't even there. DeeDee welled up. With tears in her eyes, she turned away from Trey. She didn't want him to see her cry.

"He's been like this since he had his breakfast. He hasn't uttered a word. Has he said anything to you two?" DeeDee asked.

"No, not a word, hasn't looked up from the book."

"Okay well there is no reason for me to stay here. I will leave when you both leave."

"I will stay with him for a while," Liz told her. "I have taken the rest of the day off."

"Dinner is at six, please come for dinner," she told her sister.

Will and DeeDee kissed and said goodbye to Trey.

"Okay, bye," he said, still never looking up.

"Liz, we will see you at dinner."

They left. DeeDee lost it outside of her son's room. She bawled, buried her head in her husband's chest and cried.

"I can't take this. Oh God, please heal him as I know you can," she prayed and cried. Finally, she got herself together, Will went back to work, and DeeDee headed home.

"I pray the surgery works. I want my son back but better," DeeDee was talking out loud again. Pretty soon I will be answering myself, she thought. She sat on the sofa and relaxed for a minute. She fell asleep. When she awoke, it was almost three. She jumped up, trying to get her bearings. She stretched her arms over her head and thanked God for waking her. She must start dinner.

She rang Liz to see if there had been any change in Trey. Liz answered in an upbeat almost jovial voice.

"Hey sis! How are you?"

"I am better, thank you for asking. Just checking on Trey."

"Oh, he's better. We have been playing UNO. I brought a deck with me."

"He's playing?"

"Yes, honey. Don't worry, he seems to be in a great mood," Liz assured her. "I will leave after he has eaten his dinner. I'll see you soon. Don't fret."

DeeDee hung the phone up from her sister. Mouth agape and totally astonished at what she had just heard. She was thankful for the good news, but she didn't understand. Trey had never responded to her. Now, she could start her dinner in peace. She had decided to make a stove top spinach lasagna, Liz wasn't much on meat and Will wasn't picky. She had some garlic bread in the freezer and a side salad would make for a nice dinner. Liz only drank champagne, DeeDee always kept a bottle on ice just for Liz.

Will received a call from the hospital at about ten p.m. They were watching the ten o'clock news. Will answered and it was Trey's night nurse.

"Hello, hello? may I speak with Mr. or Mrs. Wilson please?"

"This is Mr. Wilson," Will answered.

"Mr. Wilson, this is George from Mapleton Hospital."

"Yes, George, what is it?" Will asked.

"We had to sedate Trey again, he got out of bed and went into another patient's room and removed his IV. He not only removed it, but he also yanked it out of his arm. When we all ran to see what the commotion was, he was banging the patient with his fist. Blood was everywhere. We finally managed to stop him and sedate him. The doctor on duty had him moved to the eighth floor to the Psychiatric Ward."

"What time did this happen?"

"About an hour ago. We have him under control now, we needed to notify both sets of parents."

"How is the other boy?" Will asked.

"He's okay. A little shaken up, but he will be fine. A warning when you come in to see him, he has been restrained. His arms and legs have been strapped to his bed. There are other patients in his room, we can't risk this kind of thing happening again. He could have been so much worse."

"Do you need for me to come up there to the hospital?"

"No, that's not necessary, Mr. Wilson. He's under sedation, there's really nothing you can do, we had to inform you of the situation."

"Thank you for calling."

"You are quite welcome," with that the call ended. Will relayed the phone call to his wife. They cuddled and tried to resume their sleep. DeeDee went into silent prayer. Will let out a helpless sigh.

"Good night again, honey," he squeezed DeeDee tight. She didn't answer, she was in deep prayer.

Trey's surgery was scheduled, it would take place in four days. Will, DeeDee, and Liz would be there until it was over, and he was in recovery. They had a few days before their son would go under the knife. DeeDee went to visit him in the afternoon, she didn't want to go in the morning for fear that she wouldn't be able to see him tied down, Will had referred to him being restrained but any way you look at it, he was tied down. He was getting fed intravenously.

WhenDeeDee walked into to the psychiatric ward, she did not see him at first. Trey was in the last bed by the window. He could see out and watch the pigeons. He laid there like a lost child. His hair was a mess, he was restrained to the point that he couldn't move. But it was still hard to see and remember what his illness had come to. Her baby was tied down like an animal. Trey saw DeeDee coming toward him, and he tried to get up.

"Mommy, Mommy! Please, I want to go home!" He was crying, he was trying to get loose. DeeDee went over, leaned down to hug him, and he bit her ear. DeeDee jerked back, she was bleeding.

"Get me out of here, I will kill you," Trey was flailing as best he could, but the restraints didn't allow him to break free. *Thank God!* DeeDee thought, *thank God!*

The nurse came over and gave a wet cloth to put to her ear. Her earring was gone, so she told the nurse that he must have swallowed it. DeeDee went back to his bed after collecting herself. He wouldn't even look at her. DeeDee couldn't take it, so she left.

The nurse told her to go to her doctor as she may need stitches. When she got home, she found her earring in her blouse. She nursed her ear. Good thing it didn't need stitches. She noticed that after the bleeding stopped. *I will be fine, it's my child that I am concerned about.*

DeeDee took time to recuperate from the events at the hospital. Trey had gotten worse. The surgery was taking place in the morning. Time was flying by. She wanted her life to be back to normal, as normal was for her family. It was nice having Will to herself but, nonetheless, their son was missing from the home.

Oh God, my God, I pray that you take our child through a successful operation and heal his brain. Father, I ask that you make him better. All this asked in Thy will. Let Your will be done, whatever Thy will let us accept it. In Jesus name, I pray, amen.

Back at the hospital, more pictures of Trey's brain had been taken. The new pictures revealed that the mass had grown. It was attached near his pituitary gland. It produces the human growth hormone, or HGH, the hormone that regulates growth, as well as builds bones and muscles. That may be why Trey was so big for his age, they wouldn't know more until after his surgery.

Will and DeeDee would spend their last night together for a while. After the surgery, DeeDee would stay at the hospital with Trey. She had been cleared to stay in his room after he was brought back from recovery. Tomorrow was the big day.

Will made another nice dinner for the two of them. They ate, they cleaned the kitchen together, they watched the news. DeeDee didn't tell Will about the incident at the hospital. She didn't want to worry him. She gave it to God. The two retired early, they had a long stressful day tomorrow.

Will, DeeDee, and Liz arrived at the hospital early in the morning. It was 6:30 a.m. Trey was already being prepped. They went into his room before he was taken to the operating room. He seemed calm when the three entered; but as soon as he saw his parents, he began to cry. Trey was still tethered to his bed, but only his arms. His feet and legs were free. The nurses were timid, with him not having his legs constrained, he could kick if he had the notion, or if he had an episode.

When Trey began to cry, he never called for his parents, he just wept.

"I want to go home," he said. "I want to go home," he repeated.

"Yes, honey, I know, and we want you to come home," his parents reassured him that as soon as he was better, he would be able to come home.

"But mommy, I am better," he cried. "Please take me home."

Will went over closer to his bed and rubbed his forehead.

"It's going to be alright, baby boy. The doctors are going to make you better, then you will be able to go home with me and mommy," he told his child.

The nurse came to take him away. All the necessary preparations have been made that could be made on that floor. Trey would now be taken over to the operating room. They walked with him from elevator to elevator, until they reached the operating room door, where they could go no further. The nurse informed them that they could wait in the private waiting room. They could get food and bring it back, if needed, she explained. She also let them know that there were snacks and refreshments in the waiting room as well. They thanked her and she returned to Trey. She pushed through the double doors. Three stood watching until he was out of sight. When Dr. Teleflora came into the waiting room, Liz had left and said she would be back. The doctor sat down with Will and DeeDee to explain the procedures that would take place shortly.

"Mr. and Mrs. Wilson, your son is in good hands. I will be performing his surgery; however, the entire team is very capable. I won't go into full details. But I will say that we will be removing the tumor from his brain, as we have said before. The surgery should take approximately seven hours. It could go longer, so please don't be alarmed if you haven't heard from me by then. Take a deep breath and try and be patient," the doctor explained. "Will you all be staying here at the hospital?" "Yes," Will answered. DeeDee didn't speak, only sat in her chair with her head down, trying not to get too emotional. Liz would return later.

Time seemed to drag on, it had now been eighthours and fifteen minutes. They were informed that it could take longer. Another twenty minutes went by and then Dr. Teleflora walked into the room.

"He's in recovery," he said to them. "The surgery went well. We think we got it all. However, it is not a tumor at all which was we thought at first. It resembles that of another brain."

"What?" Will was shocked at what he was hearing.

"Yes, Mr. Wilson," the doctor said. "We will know more once it's been examined. The specimen from your son's head has been sent over to the pathology lab. We will know more once the results are in. It could take several days."

"Can we see our son?" asked DeeDee, "When he is out of the recovery room, you may."

"He will be placed in a room?"

"Recovery should only take about an hour, you can see him then," Doctor Teleflora assured. "When he is back in his room, he will still be sedated. We will place Trey in a medically induced coma to keep him stable. This is to protect him from any sudden movements. We tend to do this procedure in children."

"This was a serious operation, and he came through with flying colors. We want to make sure he remains still. Children tend to want to move around when they start to feel better," the doctor explained.

"When can we see him?"Liz, who has returned, asked, Liz was family and Liz was moral support..]

"I will be in my office, if you have any questions, please do not hesitate to contact either myself or my nurse," the doctor said.

They all thanked the doctor, and he was gone.

"Still more waiting," DeeDee said out loud.

"The worst is over, sis," Liz went over to give her sister a big hug.

"I know you are right, but I need to see him for myself," DeeDee explained. Her anxiety was starting to mount, but she sat with the other two and waited.

"Trey had not been assigned to a room yet," DeeDee said. "I pray that they wouldn't take him back to the psychiatric ward. That place was horrible. Patients strapped down like animals."

"They don't strap animals down," Will said to his wife. "They put them in cages. Thankfully maybe now he won't have to be placed in an institution." All agreed.

It was getting late, Liz went home. She had work early in the morning. Will would sit with his wife until they could see their son. Then DeeDee was prepared to stay the night. She had been told that there would be a cot placed in Trey's room so she would be able to stay by her sons' side if she chooses.

"I am staying," she said to Will.

"Alright, honey," Will said. "But I am not going to leave until I see him."

It was 10:30 p.m. when they finally put Trey in a room. He was not back on the psychiatric ward. He was in a private room on the third floor, in one of the two children's wards. Trey's parents entered his room and DeeDee let out a gasp and threw her hands at her face. She started to cry. Will just stood looking at his son.

Trey had a humongous bandage over his entire small head. His eyes were barely visible and there were tubes and machines everywhere. Rhythmic noises came from the machines, almost as if they were playing a song. Trey laid there, out cold and totally oblivious. Thank God, DeeDee thought, I am glad that he will be out for a while, he would not like to see all this stuff on and around him.

Will didn't want to stay any longer. He wanted to go home and have a glass of wine. He needed to take somtime for himself. He kissed DeeDee, kissed Trey's hand and left.

The hospital was only twenty minutes away, but Will thought it was take forever for him to get home. When he got settled with his glass of wine, he broke down. He did not like seeing his son like that. Will tried to reason with himself, but it wasn't working. He was a man of little faith, but he tried reasoning with God. He began to pray and believe it or not he found that he felt better, when he was done praying, he told God thank you.

Will took his wine into the living room and plopped down into his favorite chair. He turned on the TV and watched mindless television. He fell asleep. There he slept until the next morning. Upon awaking he was disoriented. Still a little groggy. He looked around the room to get his bearings before going upstairs to get ready for work. He would work half day and then head to the hospital.

Will left work around noon. His boss, Benny, thought that Will should take off until Trey started to get better. Benny said many times that his wife needed him by her side. The truth be known, Will had no desire to sit at that hospital day in and day out watching his son laying there looking like a zombie. He was trying with everything in him to be supportive, but it wasn't in him. After all, Will's take on the whole situation was to put Trey in an asylum. He was tired of the entire mess.

How and why would or could a parent think like Will was thinking? Will had said often that he wished things were the way they were before Trey. DeeDee loved her son and loved her husband. But she would be there for her son to the bitter end. You don't just have a child or children and because they are not perfect in your eyes, you toss them away. All children were perfect in the eyes of God. God has the final say in this matter. Not William Wilson. For that matter nor DeeDee Wilson. So there! DeeDee had said many times that if Will didn't want to stick it out with the two of them and he left, she would accept it, but she would not like or agree with his decision to do so.

When Will arrived at the hospital in the late afternoon, DeeDee was sitting in her favorite spot in Trey's room. In the big chair on the right side of his bed. Machines still singing, tubes still everywhere, and Trey lying in his same position. He moved as he was still in a coma. It had been 4 days since the surgery, still no news as to when Dr. Teleflora would wake him up. Apparently, Trey wasn't healing as fast as the doctors had hoped. DeeDee had been staying every night. She would go home, shower, change clothes, and go back to the hospital.

Will felt abandoned by his wife. She had not slept at home in almost a week. She needed to come home tonight. Will needed his wife. What was she there for anyway? Trey had no idea that she was there. DeeDee would beg to differ. She felt that her baby sensed her presence. Will took his wife by the hand, led her to the waiting area around the corner from Trey's room. He sat her down.

"I haven't seen much of my wife lately. I want you to come home with me," he told her. "We must sit down to a dinner for two. I will order in; you don't have to cook."

"Trey is in good hands," Will pleaded with her. "The doctors will call if anything changes."

DeeDee knew her husband was right. She had missed him too. They returned to Trey's room, said their goodbyes and left. Will was elated for however long he had his precious DeeDee.

They drove separate cars but got home close to the same time. Will arrived home minutes before DeeDee. They ordered through Hungry for Eats. It came quickly, they liked that app because they were fast and friendly. The two ate and relaxed in the living room, watched a movie, and cuddled. They were there for hours enjoying each other's company. It was time to retire for the night. They went up and prepared for bed. Will had decided that he would take some time off, when Trey was conscious again. There was no need for both of us to sit and stare.

The next day, DeeDee was sitting with Trey when there was a tap on the glass. She looked up and it was Trey's pediatrician, Dr. Thompson. She waved him in.

"How are you holding up?" he asked.

"I guess as well as can be expected," she answered DeeDee.

"I know it's been a while since the surgery, but all things considered his progress has been slow but steady. From what I have seen on his charts and from talking with the rest of the team, we should be waking him up in the next week or so. His scars are healing nicely and from the X-rays, his brain is healing well too. It looks like they got everything, but Dr. Teleflora will tell you more when he speaks with you and Mr. Wilson."

"Thank you for stopping by, doctor," said DeeDee.

"Hours later, Dr. Teleflora came by Trey's room. The two exchanged niceties.

"Is your husband coming up today?" he asked DeeDee.

"I am not sure, sir. Is there a problem?"

"No, no problem. I would like to talk to both of you," the doctor said.

"Okay then. I will call him; he can come after work."

"That will be fine," the doctor said, "Have his nurse call me when he arrives. I will be staying up late this evening, I'll be around. I will see you then."

Will arrived at six p.m..and went to see DeeDee in Trey's room. The nurse rang Dr. Teleflora, and after about thirty minutes, he walked in.

He said to them, "Do you mind if we go around to the waiting area to talk?"

"That will be fine," DeeDee and Will responded.

"Please sit down." They all sat, and the doctor began.

"The team has been monitoring your son's x-rays very carefully. It appears that we weren't able to get all the mass, which we know now for sure that it is a second brain."

"I thought that you said nothing was wrong!" DeeDee yelled at the doctor.

"I didn't want to upset you, which is why I wanted to speak to the both of you together," the doctor explained.

"Calm down, honey," Will said, pacifying his wife. "Let's hear what the doctor has to say."

"We want to go back in." Dr. Teleflora resumed. "The rest of what we did not get out is starting to grow. The part that was removed is growing as well. We have never seen a case like this before." "No! You will not cut on my child again," DeeDee said

"I understand how you must feel, but please think about it, talk it over. We would like to go back in before we bring him out of the coma."

"We will get back to you doctor," Will shook the doctor's hand. DeeDee did not say another word to him before he left.

"What do I tell him?" DeeDee uttered.

"Tell who?" Will asked her.

"What do I tell Trey?" DeeDee said.

Will looked perplexed. He had no response for her. They both left without saying goodbye to Trey. My wife is losing it, Will thought.

They thought it over. DeeDee convinced Will not to allow the second surgery. They would talk to the team about other options. But there would be no more cutting, no more surgery on his brain. The team continued to monitor him and thought it was time to bring him out of the coma. The bandages would be taken off in a week. Depending on how well he was still healing, they possibly would bring him out of the coma sooner.

Two weeks went by and apparently the growth had ceased to get any larger. The team had opted to treat the growth with steroids rather than operate again. The Wilsons wouldn't allow it anyway. The bandages had been removed and his scarring was minimal, Trey's beautiful curly head was gone. Liz was there at the hospital with them. There were lesser machines now as they had been gradually removed. Trey was breathing his own, and they were going to wake him soon. The drugs that were used intravenously were now removed. Trey would awake slowly. Everyone was there waiting to greet him. They waited with bated breath for the patient to awaken. It had been two hours when Trey began to stir. He slowly opened his eyes; he glanced about the room. He spotted his mother and then his father, his entire team was there also. Aunt Liz and Mr. Benny, Will's boss, were there. He sat up in bed as straight as an arrow.

"Mommy!" he yelled and held out his weak little arms for her to come to him. "Daddy! Auntie Liz!

They all went over for one big group hug. It was a great time to be had. Trey Allan Wilson was awake. The good Lord willing he would be well soon. He would be going to therapy for about two weeks to strengthen his bones. Rehab was across the street in the other building. He still needed to stay in the rehab facility until he regained his strength. His mom was sure he would not like that, but he would get used to it. Trey had been in the hospital for three months already, most of which he was out, a couple more weeks wouldn't be so bad.

DeeDee wasn't feeling herself lately, she told Will and he suggested she go for her checkup a few weeks early. It was time for their annual exams. She called her doctor to schedule her physical. She would be going in two days. DeeDee had been on an emotional roller coaster in the last three months. She hoped she was fine. She gave it to God. Will got his physical through his work and he checked out fine. Healthy as a horse, so to speak. Trey had been transferred to rehab and wasn't happy but getting along. DeeDee went to her annual exam and her doctor gave her the green light. It meant that on the surface she was fine. They are now only waiting for her blood test results to come back in three days. Her doctor would call if she saw any issues. That's the way it always was. The test always came back normal.

DeeDee was home making dinner, Trey was in rehab and Will was still at work when the phone rang.

"Hello," she answered.

"Hi, DeeDee," the person on the other line greeted. "This is Doctor Princeton, your primary care physician."

"Hello, doc. Is something wrong?" she asked.

"Well, that's a question you must answer." DeeDee was not following her.

"Okay, I won't beat around the bush," the doctor continued. "DeeDee, you and Will are pregnant."

DeeDee dropped the phone, but she gathered herself after a few seconds.

"Are you sure?" she asked her doctor.

"Positive! You are nine weeks along. Congratulations, my dear. I will set up your next appointment a week from now. You will be ten weeks by then. I will see you soon." With that, she hung up.

DeeDee sat reeling from the news. They had been trying for years to get pregnant again. Admittedly, they didn't use protection. They had decided that if it happened, it happened. "God works in mysterious ways," she said aloud. "In his time, not in ours."

Maybe this is what Trey needed, a sister or a brother, she thought.

DeeDee couldn't wait to tell her husband. She would go back to the hospital, visit Trey for a while, then go home and make dinner. She would break the news over a nice dinner. She couldn't stay with Trey in rehab overnight anyway. Just perfect, she thought to herself.

When DeeDee visited Trey, she observed that he was progressing nicely. He had only been in rehabilitative therapy for two days and was already showing great promise. When DeeDee entered the rehab center, Trey was walking on a tiny treadmill. It wasn't so tiny at all, it just looked like that from afar. Trey saw his mother and lost his focus. He slipped and fell. DeeDee ran over to help him up, but his therapist threw up his hand to stop her.

Trey's therapist's name was Thomas, he had been in the field for eleven years. He was thirty-two years old, with a master's degree, not married, and no children. Thomas only worked with children by choice. He followed Trey after meeting DeeDee.

"He must do this on his own," Thomas explained to her. "There may be a fall here and there; but remember, this place is designed for safety. Everything we do here is for the good of our patients. At the rate Trey is going, he may not need the full two weeks."

"I understand," DeeDee said, and began explaining. "It's just that he had been away from us, his father and I, for over three months. I apologize, it was a mother's instinct."

"I understand," Thomas told her. "We need to be on the same page though."

"We are," DeeDee responded.

When Trey was finished with his session, he was taken back to his room, with DeeDee in tow. He was put in his wheelchair to have his lunch. He was in his wheelchair most of the day. He was allowed to roll himself around his room and down the hall. This would help with the strengthening his arms. Thankfully, his muscles hadn't atrophied because he had been getting therapy several times a day. So far, there had been no outbursts and no new growth in his brain. Trey was doing great. His team was over the moon with how far he had come. They had even discussed the possibility of his journey becoming an article in the Mapleton Medical magazine.

DeeDee sat with Trey until four o'clock. She was going home to start dinner. She had brought Trey several books and homework to keep him busy. Trey also had his Nintendo with some of his games. He had gotten his game player for his sixth birthday. DeeDee gave him a kiss and prepared to leave. For the first time since he was in the hospital, he let her leave without incident.

He said, "Okay, mommy. See you tomorrow."

DeeDee smiled and told him, "Yes, you will, my sweet boy." She left.

When she got home, she took a minute to take in what Dr. Thompson had told her. She rubbed her stomach and saidy a prayer.

"Thank you so much, God. This is all a part of your plan. I receive and accept it with arms wide open. I pray that you will continue to heal our son and our family. Please keep us all safe. In Jesus name, I pray. Amen."

She went into the kitchen with pep in her step and a song in her heart. Elated at the news, she had hoped that Will would be as happy as she was. Of course, he would, why wouldn't he be? This was what we had been hoping for and she had been praying for.

She was humming and dancing around the kitchen, all while making dinner. She set the table with candles and a vase with fresh flowers. There were two wine glasses, but one, would only have cranberry juice. She didn't want to give anything away; so, Will would have his favorite red wine. She made baked pork chops, creamed spinach, red cabbage, and roasted potatoes, all Will's favorites.

When cooking dinner was finished, DeeDee went upstairs to take a shower and get dressed. She put on a lovely blue dress; blue was her best color. Will also liked this blue dress. When she was dressed, she looked at herself in the mirror, and was pleased with what she saw. She heard Will come in; he called her when he saw that she wasn't in the kitchen.

"Up here, honey. Be down in a minute."

"Okay, I'll wash up for dinner," he yelled back to her.

The table was already set so there was nothing left to do but put dinner on the table. She came down and Will was in his favorite chair in front of the TV watching the six o'clock news. She walked over and sat on his lap.

"Wow! You look and smell delicious. My beautiful wife, I love you," he told her. He snuck a kiss; she grabbed him by the hand and led him to the dining room table.

"So, what do I owe the dining room dinner? Did something happen today with Trey?" he asked. They usually ate in the kitchen unless it was a special occasion.

"Trey is moving right along with his therapy," DeeDee shared. She served dinner, with the glasses filled already. She did that to not stir any suspicions from her having juice. She blessed the food, and the couple began eating.

"I have a surprise," DeeDee announced. "But it would need to wait until after the dishes are cleared, cleaned, and put away."

So the copule did that together. After that was accomplished, DeeDee led her husband into the sofa in the living room. She threw her legs over him, looked him in the eyes and spoke.

"We are with child. As in, we are pregnant, a baby in the oven, all the above. Take your pick," she said with a big grin.

Will stared at her if she were a strange object or something. He did not speak for a good minute. Then, when he finally found the words, he said, "What did you just say? Did I hear you correctly? Are you making jokes right now?"

"No, honey, you heard me right. We are going to have another child."

Tears welled up in his eyes, he kissed his wife, put his head in the crook of her neck and sobbed.

DeeDee finally said, "I hope those are happy tears."

"Of course, they are," Will replied through a river of tears. "Oh, honey, this is the best news since in forever. I am so thankful."

Will looked to the ceiling and screamed, "Thank you, God! Thank you!"

The two sat in silence for quite some time, he looked at her and told her that he loved her more than life itself. They retired for the evening, loving life again. Trey was getting better, and he was going to be a big brother. They laid down and talked about making plans for the nursery. There was a guest room that would be perfect. They would convert it together. They talked until drifting off to sleep.

The next day was as usual; however, breakfast was different, Will could not stop grinning. DeeDee could not keep her hands off her husband as well. They ended up back upstairs in bed.

"You are going to be late, William," she scolded him.

"Benny won't mind when I tell him the news," Will reasoned.

DeeDee gave him a to-go cup of coffee and pushed him out of the door. She cleaned up and left for the hospital.

When DeeDee arrived at the hospital, Trey wasn't in his room. It was too early for him to be down the hall in rehab. She was leaving his room when the nurse came in to see her.

"Where is Trey?" DeeDee asked the nurse.

"Mrs. Wilson, he is back upstairs in the psychiatric ward. He had an explosive episode about an hour ago. He had to be restrained again. Dr. James did not want to sedate him, so he ordered him back to confinement."

DeeDee felt faint, the nurse helped her over to a chair and brought her a glass of water.

"I don't understand, he was doing so well," said DeeDee, weary.

"For whatever reason, he must have relapsed," the nurse explained. "The doctor will be in to talk with you soon."

"Okay, thank you. I will sit and wait for him. I must call my husband."

There was no way that they could tell Trey about the pregnancy. That may only make things worse for him. DeeDee rang Will at work, he answered in a panic.

"Honey, are you alright? Is something wrong?"

"Trey had a relapse," she explained. "He is back on that god-awful ward. I haven't been to see him yet; do you think that we should hold off telling him about the baby?"

"Yes, I think we should wait, at least until we talk to the doctor," Will agreed.

"I really hate to pull you away from work, but I think you should come," said DeeDee.

She waited for her husband in Trey's room, just sitting there with a blank stare. She didn't move until she saw Will come through the door. She ran over to him and hugged him around his neck.

"The doctor is on his way," she told him. "He will meet us in the private waiting room."

The two waited patiently. When the doctor arrived, he sat down in the chair next to them.

"Mr. and Mrs. Wilson, I really hate to be the barer of bad news, but your son is still mentally unstable," he began explaining.

"The portion of the other brain that was removed show signs of a deformity. It can be treated with medication; however, we don't think that he should be returning to your home. We think it would be best to have him transferred to Mapleton Mental Asylum.

"I don't want you to decide right now, go home and think about it. Come back tomorrow. I also don't think it's wise for you to see him right now. He was making threats against you both."

DeeDee passed out. Will laid her out on the sofa of the waiting room while the doctor called for the nurse. They revived her and wanted to give her a sedative, but Will said not to since she is pregnant.

"It is only a mild sedative; it won't hurt her or the baby. There is some good to come from this," the doctor said. "Congratulations to you both. So sorry for the bad news."

Then, the doctor left the waiting room. DeeDee refused the sedative. She would call her obstetrician, Dr. Thomson. After the call, the doctor gave her a referral to Dr. Maas.

Will Took DeeDee home, he left her car because he didn't want her to drive.

"I will call Liz when we get back home, she can come with me to pick up your car later. It's safe where it's parked," Will said to DeeDee.

When they arrived home, DeeDee called Dr. Maas to see if she could get an immediate appointment to see her. She had relayed the issues at hand. Dr. Maas was an obstetrician-gynecologist and was a friend and colleague of her primary care doctor.

Since DeeDee needed an appointment as soon as possible, Dr. Maas gave her an appointment for two p.m. that same day. That was perfect, Will had already left work so he would accompany her. DeeDee rang Liz to update her on Trey; however, she did not mention her condition. Will had only told his boss. They had originally decided to have a small get-together to break the news. But after receiving the news about Trey, they would maybe have to postpone or not have it at all.

DeeDee and Will arrived at Dr. Maas' office a few minutes early. She had to fill out forms, which took several minutes. When she was done it was ten past two o'clock, so she was able to go right in to see her new doctor.

Dr. Maas way a pretty woman, mid-forties, and tall at about five feet and ten inches. She appeared to be very fit. She had dark brown hair down to her waist and had it pulled back with a headband. Once the introductions were exchanged, a nurse came in to give DeeDee a gown. The nurse explicitly told her that the opening should be in the front. Will was standing right by her side, observing.

When DeeDee was ready for her exam, the doctor returned.

"You are in good health," Dr. Maas told her. "I want to prescribe a mild sedative for you to take as needed. It won't harm the baby. But you are going through a lot right now. If you start to feel too overwhelmed, take one pill."

"If you feel you can handle things on your own, that's fine. I want you to make an appointment for two weeks from now and we will do a sonogram. Are you going to wait to know the sex?"

"Not sure," Will chimed in. "Our other child is very sick; our focus must be on him now and also keeping my wife healthy so the new baby will be healthy as well."

"I hear you, Mr. Wilson, and I agree 100 percent. Please call me if you need to."

"Will, our poor boy," DeeDee sighed. "What are we going to do?"

"I am with his team of doctors; he should be in an asylum," said Will.

"That's nothing new, that's what you've always wanted," she told him. They remained quiet all the way home.

"I don't feel like cooking, you can order in," DeeDee said.

"Okay, what do you have a taste for?" asked Will.

"I want sardines and vanilla ice cream."

"Sardines? You hate even the smell of those foul little fish," Will was surprised.

"I know, so I guess we know that the cravings have begun," DeeDee answered.

"We may as well tell her," countered DeeDee.

In the end, they agreed they would tell Liz the news, all of it, when she came over to take Will to get her car. "We will call her later in the week."

The topic concerning what to do about Trey kept the couple on each other's neck.

"We can't have him locked away. We are having another child, and he should be here to be a part of it," DeeDee reasoned.

"He is not sane honey; the doctor broke it down today," answered Will.

"What if we asked the doctor about bringing him home with medications? Anyway, he won't be anywhere near coming home until he finishes his rehab," she told him.

"Okay, baby, how in the world will he be able to finish rehab if he's tethered to a bed?" Will was trying to rationalize with DeeDee.

"The same way they will maybe medicate him so that he can come home."

"You are not listening," said Will, exasperated.

"You are also not hearing anyone," DeeDee answered back.

Somehow the media got wind of Trey's condition. They had information on his surgery, as well as the second brain. The brain that hadn't been talked about since his surgery. Where was the brain? Why hadn't the team mentioned it since they had removed it. How did the media get wind of any of this? These were the questions in DeeDee's mind. Questions to be asked and answered. And soon.

In the meantime, Will didn't go to work and took two weeks of FMLA. He realized they needed to resolve some things. He also needed to be there for his wife and son. He had to convince his wife that Trey would be better off in the hospital and that there was no other way. He decided to talk to Liz and get another perspective. Liz was the oldest sister; she kept a level head about everything. She didn't do anything before weighing the pros and cons. She didn't get to the top of her game by making snap decisions. Will thought that the three of them would sit down and figure things out. But before he could bring Liz on board, DeeDee would need to be convinced as well. That's why Will needed to talk to his wife after dinner that night.

The couple still had not seen Trey. DeeDee was out of her wits, she wanted to visit her son. It had been three days since she or Will had laid eyes on him. She learned that the nurses had taken him out of his restraints, but he had been heavily medicated. His feet were still tethered to his bed. The nurse had explained his current condition to them when they called. DeeDee asked if Trey had called for his mother or his father. She told her no, that Trey had not spoken in a few days. His last spoken words were threats.

The doctors were giving him a host of drugs. The only way to keep Trey calm was to medicate him. They didn't want to sedate him because they needed him to be awake. He was always under a microscope. They were perplexed by this seven-year-old child.

Will and DeeDee called Liz over for dinner. The couple had decided that they would sit down and let Liz in on all that had taken place in the last three days, which seemed like a lifetime. Liz agreed to come for dinner. And by five p.m., there was a knock on the door, Will thought it was Liz, so he opened the door. Instead, it was a reporter.

Will slammed the door in the reporter's face after he told him that if he didn't get off his property, he would call the police. The reporter quickly left.

"Is that Liz, honey?" DeeDee asked.

No, it was a reporter, now they know where we live," He let out a frustrated sigh.

There was another knock on the door. Will snatched the door open, ready for the reporter, but it was Liz.

"Oh my! What's wrong?" Liz asked. "You invited me, but did I come at a bad time?"

"Reporters," Will explained.

"Why are reporters coming here?" she asked. Then Will explained about Trey's condition getting out to the pressWhen they all finally sat down for dinner, Will and Liz had wine glasses while DeeDee had a gobbler. Liz looked over at her sister.

"You're not drinking tonight?" Liz asked her sister.

"No, it will be a while before I drink again."

Will took the liberty to start the discussion." Liz," he said, "we are expecting."

Liz jumped from her chair and went over to give her sister a big hug. "Congratulations to you both. Does Trey know yet?"

"No, he doesn't," Will said to Liz. "Trey is back in lock-up, tied down and totally confined right now. He had another episode this morning and they transferred him back to psych ward. They want to put him in an asylum."

"Oh no!" Liz put her hand to her mouth and became very emotional.

"That's why we wanted you to come over, we want your opinion," Will said to his sister-in-law.

"What, you want me to chime in on what you should do concerning Trey?" clarified Liz.

"Yes, Liz, we want your thoughts on it," confirmed Will.

"Well, my friends that is not going to happen. I love you all, but this decision must be between the two of you," Liz took a gulp of her wine and sat back in her chair, looking from Will to DeeDee.

"I will not be a part of any choice to put him away or not put him away," she said emphatically. "Is there no other way?"

"He possibly would be able to come home with medication, but Will thinks it's best if he goes away," DeeDee revealed. "I am expecting, and he feels that it would be far too much for me to handle."

"What do you want or think, Sis?" asked Liz.

"I want him to come home if there is any way possible, I want him home," said DeeDee firmly.

They ate in silence; they drank in silence. It was getting late, and Liz wanted to go home.

"I am leaving. I will ring you tomorrow, Sis. Have a good night," Liz said goodbye.

DeeDee walked her sister to the door and said good night. DeeDee cleared the table, cleaned the kitchen, and then she and Will went up to bed with no more conversation on the subject. Will and DeeDee climbed into bed and turned their separates ways, backs to each other, and went to sleep. There was no mention of Liz picking up DeeDee's car.

The next morning was the same, filled with silence. There was very little conversation between the two. They ate breakfast, then headed to the hospital. Will broke the ice in the car and said to DeeDee, "Honey, we will talk to the doctor today. And if we can be reassured that if he has meds that work, then we will bring him home."

"Really, honey, you mean it?" DeeDee wanted to be sure.

"Yes, if that's what you want."

"That's what I want," she affirmed. "Thank you, sweetheart. He should be home with us." Will never responded.

They arrived at the hospital at 10 a.m. and took the elevators to the eighth floor. DeeDee hated that floor. All the children were zombies. Sedated and tethered to their beds. The nurse met them at the door of Trey's room.

"Before you go in, I want to make you aware that he has been out for about an hour," the nurse explained. "We had no choice but to sedate him. He had another manic episode. The restraints were irritating his wrist, so we loosened them. But he still fought against them. The doctor wants to have a word with you, before you leave."

"That's fine. We will sit with Trey. Hopefully we can say hello before we leave," said DeeDee.

The psychiatrist came in to speak with the Wilsons. He escorted them to the waiting room down the hall.

"I am going to be blunt; you must not take him home. He is dangerous, to himself and others," Dr. Teleflora advised.

"He is going home as soon as he is well enough," DeeDee said to Dr. Teleflora.

"If that is your decision, then so be it," the doctor said.

"We want him to get better and finish with rehab before we take him, doctor," Will told him.

"Yes, if we can get his outbursts under control, he will be able to return to rehab."

"Thank you, doctor," DeeDee said, and they returned to Trey's room, where their child had begun to stir, now just waking up.

"Mommy, daddy," he tried to reach out his hand, but he was unable to.

They walked over to his bed, one on either side and both held his hand.

"I want to go home. Please take me home," he pleaded.

"Honey, we are going to take you home, but you must get better," DeeDee coaxed her child. "Please try and be patient." Telling a seven-year-old boy to be patient, next to impossible.

Days went by and Trey had begun to show significant improvement. The cocktail of medications appeared to be working. Trey was back in rehab and on his way to a full recovery. They still had not told Trey of the baby.

DeeDee's sonogram appointment was also fast approaching. Trey was getting better; things were starting to look up for the Wilson family. Will remained on FMLA until they got Trey home and settled. Their next step was to hire another home care nurse. The two of them would interview the new prospect together.

More days had gone by with no recent episodes from Trey. DeeDee was scheduled to have her sonogram and Will came with her. They arrived at Dr. Maas' office early. The waiting room was full, more than likely she would still need to wait. DeeDee checked in at the front desk and she and Will waited to be called.

"Mrs. Wilson," the nurse called her back. Dr. Maas walked in at four p.m. looking as fresh as a daisy.

"Hello, you two. Are we ready to look and hear a heartbeat?" the doctor asked.

"Overly excited," the couple responded almost at the same time.

Dr. Maas placed the cold gel on DeeDee's stomach, followed by the colder transducer. They immediately heard not one but two sets of thumps.

"Oh, my goodness," exclaimed Dr. Maas. "There are twins inside that tummy!"

"Twins?" DeeDee cried out.

"Yes, Mrs. Wilson, you are having two little bundles," the doctor confirmed.

Will was grinning from ear to ear; in fact, they both were.

"Those two little heartbeats were very strong. They are healthy, and you two must be ecstatic."

"Yes, we are, doctor," they both said in unison.

"Well congratulations to you both. I will see you in one month. You can pick up your prenatal vitamins on your way out. I will have your next appointment scheduled and the nurse will give you a call."

They left the doctor's office on cloud nine.

"I am so happy honey; this has been a long time coming. I cannot wait to tell Trey," DeeDee told Will. "He will be so happy too; he is going to be a big brother."

"We won't say anything until he comes home," Will added.

DeeDee was in her first trimester. She was not feeling sick anymore; however, her cravings had shot off the radar. Will only sighs when his wife would ask for crazy combinations of foods. She rarely ate the same thing as he did for dinner. But that was okay with him. They were pregnant with not one but two buns in the oven. For their next doctor's visit, they said that they wanted to know the sex of their babies, if it was possible, so that there will be no more surprises. Will Laughed and gave DeeDee a big hug and a kiss before going into the house.

DeeDee made breakfast before they left for the hospital. It was the day to visit the agency to inquire about potential home care nurses. The agency was in the building across the street. Ms. Jeffery gave them information on three of their highest qualified nurses, excluding Nurse Rita Collins.

She was not a good fit. Trey made that very clear. Will thanked Ms. Jeffery and then they headed to see Trey. Trey was back on one of the regular children's wards. He was doing very well. There was never any more mention of the brain that had been removed from Trey's head four months ago. It was not a topic that anyone wanted to concern themselves with any longer. They only wanted their son to remain well and continue that path. Thank God! DeeDee prayed.

When they entered Trey's room he was in his usual place. His wheelchair. Soon, he would no longer need the chair because he was walking pretty much on his own, most of the time. Sometimes, he would tire out, so the nurse left it in his room for additional support. Trey saw his mom and dad enter and he told them to wait by the door. He wanted to show them how well he was doing. He rose from the wheelchair, steadied himself and began to walk to his parents. When he reached them, he fell into his father's arms.

Such a wonderful feeling, Will thought to himself. He later told DeeDee how good it felt to hold Trey in his arms.

Trey was quite the chatterbox. He went on and on, telling his parents of how many friends he had made, and he was looking forward to having sleepovers when he was able to go home. Trey seemed like another child. He no longer appeared to be introverted. So good to see this new side of the boy who had been so sick, and now on the road to recovery.

Thank you, Lord, DeeDee looked to the ceiling and raised her hands. Trey started to tire a bit, so he climbed in bed and his mother and father proceeded to tuck him. Just as if he were home in his own bed. There were several books that DeeDee and Liz had brought to the hospital over time. DeeDee had Trey choose one for his bedtime story. Before she was done reading, Trey was fast asleep.

The two of them eased out. Will thought of DeeDee's car down in the garage. He would call Liz when they got home to arrange for her to go with her to pick it up. The ride home was blissful. The day had been a great day. No issues or concerns. DeeDee didn't like using the word worry. She preferred issues or concerns, she thought that they are less harsh.

The two ate dinner in the living room, which was rarely practiced. DeeDee retrieved the sofa tables from the dining room closet and placed one for herself and one for Will. Liz would be over later, but she wasn't coming for dinner. She occasionally came by to check on her favorite couple. DeeDee took the dishes to the kitchen and replaced the tables in their rightful place. She then sat with Will. She decided she would clean the kitchen after they went over the resumes.

Going over the resumes, they came across one that really struck their interest. Nurse Rita's resume had peeked several of her interest as well. But Will had not been available to work with DeeDee to help her decide about Nurse Rita Collins.

Another candidate was Carmen Worthington. Age 32, single mother, one daughter aged elevent, graduated from nursing school at the age of 24, employed at Chillforth Nursing Agency for eight years. Like that of Rita Collins but for the fact that Rita had no children of note. If the interview went well and Trey liked her, then she would be their new healthcare Nurse. DeeDee decided to call her in the morning to set up an appointment at the café in the hospital. If all went well, Carmen and DeeDee would go over to rehab and meet Trey. Sounded like a solid plan.

Liz came to the house just after the two had finished making the decision about Carmen. Liz made a point of letting them know that she just dropped by for a few minutes, and she wouldn't be staying long.

She rested her purse and Will brought her a glass of wine while he had one to join her.

"So how are things?" Liz asked as she took a sip from her glass.

"Things are getting better," DeeDee replied. "Oh, before I forget Liz, I need to know if you can go with Will one day this week and retrieve my car from the hospital parking lot. It's been there for a while. I have been getting car sick lately. I am sure it's because of the babies."

Babies went right over Liz's head. She went on to say, "Well, of course, I will. You name the day, Will," Liz told her brother-in-law.

Will and DeeDee glanced at each other, waiting for babies to click in but he hadn't so far.

"Liz, did you hear what I said?" asked DeeDee.

"Yes, I heard you said, and I said I am fine with going with Will to pick up your car," answered Liz.

DeeDee smiled, "I know you are a little slow so I will come right out with it. We are having twins!"

Liz didn't respond right away but when she did, she let out a scream that could be heard at the hospital.

"Are you two serious right now? Are you serious?" She couldn't believe her ears. "Come on, you two, group hug!"

They hugged and danced around the living room. Liz was so happy. Liz knew that Will and DeeDee had given up on trying, but they had wanted more children. It was the best news ever. Liz finished her wine, said her goodbyes, and retreated to her car.

"I love you two. Bye!" she was off.

Will and DeeDee went straight to see Trey after breakfast. He was in rehab. His bed was empty, but they sat for a few minutes. Then, it was time for their meeting with Nurse Carmen. They left Trey's room and took the elevator to the basement, where the café was located. Carmen had described what she would be wearing. DeeDee spotted her immediately. Carmen waved them over to the table where she was sitting. She stood up when they arrived. They all exchanged greetings and sat for the interview. The interview lasted forty-five minutes, they were both very impressed with her.

Carmen stood about five feet and five inches tall, she was not a thin woman, but she appeared to be fit. She had a small afro, with hazel eyes and she was very pretty. DeeDee thought that it doesn't matter if she was the perfect candidate so far. They'll need Trey to accept her first, and then decide it was a match.

When all three entered Treys' room, he was back from rehab and was now sitting in his chair. He looked a bit puzzled, but he didn't speak. They approached his bed and Carmen introduced herself.

DeeDee spoke first. "Nurse Carmen is going to be your nurse when you come home."

"But mommy, I don't need a nurse!" cried Trey.

"Well, baby, you will for a little while. It will be fine honey; you will like her you'll see."

"Okay, mommy, if you say so," he said.

"Hello, Nurse Carmen," Trey stuck out his hand, "It's nice to meet you."

"Hello Trey, it's very nice to meet you too," greeted Carmen.

She then turned to them and said, "I will see you all soon."

"I will ring you when he is discharged, Carmen," DeeDee told her.

"I look forward to it," she waved goodbye to Trey and left.

"I like her mommy," Trey said.

Will had blended into the wall. He just stood back and watched.

"I am happy that you like her baby," DeeDee said to her son. "She has a daughter, maybe you will get to meet her as well."

"I hope so, I like kids," he whispered, as if he didn't want anyone else to hear.

This was not the same boy as a month ago, Will thought.

Trey's nurse came into his room and asked if she could speak with them in the hall. The couple looked perplexed.

"Of course," they said. Then the nurse led them out.

"I thought I needed to let you know that there has been a lady coming here to visits Trey," the nurse shared. "She never enters his room; she stands so that he can't see her."

"What!" Will shouted.

"Please lower your voice, Mr. Wilson," the nurse, Nurse Tina, who had been Trey's day nurse all the while on his return to children's ward, told him. "He mustn't hear us."

Nurse Tina described the woman. And it fitted Nurse Rita Collins' description, the couple saw on the applications.

"But why was she spying on our son?" Will was adamant. "Please, if she returns, or should I say when she returns, call security. We don't want him to have another episode. We don't want her anywhere near him."

Tina understood and she would pass it on.

They went to Trey's room to finish their visit. Deedee decided she would stay the night. She would go home to prepare something for Will, and he would bring her back. Meanwhile DeeDee called the agency since she tried to call the number that she had for Rita and found that it was disconnected. The agency told her that Rita had been fired, she was under investigation. Their HR said they couldn't disclose any information because of the ongoing case. DeeDee was terrified, and so was Will.

"Let's tell Trey we are going home, and I will stay with him tonight, so I will be back," DeeDee decided.

Trey was so happy. He could hardly wait for his mommy to return.

Someone named Agent Morrow from the FBI was assigned to Rita Collins' case. Rita was a total fraud. Rita was not her real name either. Her real name was Shelia Monture, she was forty-one years old. She looked very young for her age, so he assumed she was in her thirties. Shelia had red hair and Rita did not, that was no biggie because a lot of women dye their hair all the time. Shelia had stolen the name Rita Collins from a dead woman's grave. Shelia had gone under the knife; her face had been reconfigured to a small degree. She had been on the FBI's radar for a year. She was a criminal of the worst kind. Rita, aka Shelia, was on the run.

Rita was wanted for child kidnapping, bank fraud, wire fraud, money laundering, elder abuse, impersonating a dead person, and a host of other charges. If convicted, she would spend the rest of her life in prison. No one knows how long exactly; however, she had to have been working under her assumed name for at least ten years. She was dangerous, the authorities needed to get her off the street. DeeDee returned to the hospital to be with Trey as soon as possible. Will would be fine for a night or so. She wanted to catch Rita Collins, or whatever her name, spying on her son. Trey was waiting patiently for his mom. They were having a grand time playing UNO. He would have his lessons today. DeeDee would resume his home schooling whenever she stayed with him for a period. They enjoyed being together. She loved having her son back.

Will and Liz Went to retrieve DeeDee's car and take it back home. Liz returned to work and Will went to the hospital to sit with DeeDee and Trey until dinner time. He also was very happy to have his son back.

Two of the doctors from Trey's team, Dr. Thompson and his primary care doctor at the hospital, came into his room. They were glad to see both parents.

"Good afternoon," the two doctors greeted the Wilsons.

"It is so good to see you both. Really, a pleasure considering the circumstances," Dr. Thompson said. "We are thinking that Trey will be able to return home in a couple of days."

"Yes!" yelled Trey.

"Now that's great news, Doctor," Will chimed, DeeDee followed suit. "Wonderful news."

"We would like to have him come into my office at least once a week for a few months, and to visit Dr. Teleflora, who is his psychiatrist," continued Dr. Thompson. "We'll have our offices schedule his appointments and give you a call. You will be notified of his discharge date directly."

The Wilsons exchanged niceties and shook everyone's hands, and then the doctors left.

No news from the peek-a-boo, Nurse Rita Collins. The nurse said she hadn't been in today; she may have somehow gotten wind snooping on Trey. The police were searching for her, and hopefully she would be caught. Will and DeeDee were uncomfortable with her being out there. One never knows what she has in mind.

The past few days had flown by. Trey was being discharged from the hospital. DeeDee had fresh clothes and shoes for him. Will was happy to be their chauffeur. DeeDee notified Nurse Carmen of the good news. She agreed to meet them at the house. Nurse Carmen's hours were nine a.m. until three-thirty p.m., Monday through Friday unless she was needed on weekends. And in that case, she was happy to make the extra money. She had informed Will and DeeDee that if they needed her on days other than her regular Mondays to Fridays, she would need to bring her daughter, Shanna since she doesn't have a babysitter during weekends. Although sometimes she could get family to watch Shanna for the time she was working.

They all arrived at home, Trey jumped out of the car and ran to the front door, anxious to go to his room. He had been away for almost five months. When Will opened the door, Trey said hello to the house, and ran upstairs to his room. It was just the way he left it. He didn't remember destroying his room before he left. No one wanted him to recall any of the before. It might stir up bad memories. This was a fresh start for the Wilson household.

Soon after they had gotten settled, Nurse Carmen rang the doorbell. They both, Will and DeeDee, greeted her together. Trey was still up in his room. Nurse Carmen only came for a trail run since Will would be home for a few more days. Nurse Carmen will officially start on Monday.

"Trey!" Will called him to the living room. Trey responded promptly. He stood next to his mom, hugging her around her waist.

"Do you remember Nurse Carmen from the hospital?" asked DeeDee.

Trey answered his mother directly.

"Yes, I remember her, but I am not going back to that place," he told them very matter of fact.

"Oh, no honey, she will be coming here to help me during the week when your dad returns to work." Trey didn't speak, only turned and ran back to his room.

None of them knew how to respond. Nurse Carmen shrugged her shoulders, DeeDee threw her hand to her head, and Will headed to talk to his son.

"Please be gentle," DeeDee said to him.

"That was very rude, this cannot be tolerated, honey," Will said.

"We will get this straightened out," DeeDee told Nurse Carmen.

"Okay, Mrs. Wilson," the new nurse replied.

"No! Please call me DeeDee."

"Alright then, DeeDee. I will see you on Monday, give me a call if anything changes," Carmen bade her goodbye.

"Will do and thank you for taking the time to come by today," said DeeDee.

Carmen was gone. DeeDee was afraid to take the short trek upstairs to Trey's room. But she ventured out and saw what was going on. The door was closed. DeeDee knocked before entering, she turned the knob and went in. Will and Trey were sitting on his bed, chatting like father and son.

"Everything is fine, honey. He's looking forward to meeting Carmen's daughter soon," Will assured DeeDee. "He will be fine; he is just glad to be back home."

DeeDee breathed a sigh of relief. "Okay then I will leave you two to your day."

DeeDee went to start her chores. She had not been focused totally for some time. The house was always neat, but it was due for some much-needed cleaning. She was up for the task. Then, later she would start dinner after her tasks were completed. It was nice having both her boys home. It was nice just being home. DeeDee was beginning to show a tiny bit, she was still able to get into her regular clothes. She rubbed her tummy and smiled. Two babies, I wonder what you are? DeeDee thought happily to herself.

It was getting close to four p.m. and the doorbell rang. She went to the door.

"Who is it?" she asked before looking through the peephole.

There were two men in suits outside on the porch. She didn't have a clue as to who they were or what they wanted. She did not open the door, she asked again, "Who is it on the intercom?"

"We are from the FBI, we would like to talk to you please," the men declared.

"Just a minute," she called back. "I will get my husband."

DeeDee went to the bottom of the stairs and called out to Will.

"Would you come here for a sec, please?" Will trotted down the stairs as jovial as could be.

"Will, there are two FBI agents at the door," He went to the door, peeped out, then opened the door.

"May I help you?" Will asked.

The two men flashed their badges. "We want to talk to you about someone who was in your hire. Rita Collins."

"Honey, I will talk to them outside," Will said to his wife. He closed the door and stepped out onto the porch. Will offered the outdoor seats.

"What is this all about, agents?" he began.

The two FBI agents were Agent Phil Michaels and Agent John Watson. And they were looking for Rita Collins and they also explained why.

"Have you been in touch with Ms. Collins?" one of the agents asked.

"She was interviewed by my wife some months ago. I have never met her; however, she was believed to have been at the hospital, where my son was about a week prior," Will shared to the detectives. "She was never hired because of my son's reaction to her being here. In fact, he went into the hospital immediately after her visit here."

"Thank you for your time, sir," Agent Michaels said. "Here is my card. If you hear from her, please give me a call."

"Yes, I will," said Will.

Rita Collins was sitting in her car across the street, watching everything. She couldn't hear what they were saying, but she knew who they were.

Will went back in the house and relayed to DeeDee what was going on, she was in shock.

"The FBI, what on earth?" she asked Will.

"They didn't go into detail; however, they said for us to be aware that she is wanted, he said call us if she shows up here."

"Why on earth would she show up here?"

"Same question, why did she show up at the hospital?" the couple asked themselves.

Unbeknownst to them, Shelia, aka Rita, had been in a mental facility when she was seventeen and stayed there for several years.

DeeDee was preparing dinner, Will was in his chair watching the news. Trey was in his room doing Trey things, as happy as a clam.

Will called to his wife, "Honey, come here!"

She went into the living room, glanced at the TV, and she did a double take. It was Rita's face plastered on the screen. The caption wanted by the FBI. They listened to the report and were horrified at what they were hearing. DeeDee told Will to make sure that the security alarm and cameras in their home were working properly.

"Of course, they are, honey," he told her. "No worries. I am home until Monday, then Carmen will be here with you and Trey. If you don't want me to go back to work, I won't but I need to save some FMLA for when the babies arrive."

"I know, it's fine, we will be fine," DeeDee said. The conversation ceased until Trey went to bed. Will turned to the sports channel. He didn't want his son to come down and see her face on the TV. Things were going great and God-willing they would stay that way.

Dinner was great. DeeDee made their favorite meal, fried chicken. And this time mashed potatoes and kale. Trey loved his mother's kale. Trey maintained his position in the kitchen helping his mother. She and Trey cleared the table, cleaned the dishes, and they both put them away. It soon would be time for Trey to shower and get ready for bed. But in the meantime, he could go back to his room to his Trey stuff.

Will sat with DeeDee, and they watched Jeopardy. It was one of their favorite shows. They thought they were smart; however, not smart enough to try out. It was a challenge for both. They watched to learn and to find out just how much they didn't know. It was fun and something for them to do together. DeeDee adored her husband, he was a good man and a good father. She thanked God all the time for him. Will loved his wife more than life itself. They both loved their son; they didn't realize how much until he had gotten bad off mentally.

DeeDee went upstairs to Trey to get him ready for bed. There was no reason for Will and DeeDee to retire early because they didn't have to go anywhere the next day. Tomorrow is Friday. The three would find something to do together. Trey was on the floor playing with his electric train set. He had gotten it last Christmas. His eighth birthday was in two months. Trey was a September baby. DeeDee had a due date of March twenty-three, give or take. Her birthday was in May, and Will was born in June.

DeeDee got Trey settled down, Will came in and they both tucked him in, just like old times. Usually, DeeDee read him a story but on his first night back home, Will would take part. Trey was asleep before his head hit the pillow. They eased out of his room and closed the door. Seemed as though nothing had been amiss.

When Will went out early in the morning to get the paper, he noticed a strange car sitting across the street. There was no one in it, it was probably a visitor of one of the neighbors. He paid no mind. He picked up the paper and went back into the house. It was already a hot July morning. Will loved the summer. He was not fond of the cold at all. On the other hand, DeeDee would rather be cold than hot any day. Opposites attract, at least that's what they say, Will thought. DeeDee awakened and found that her husband wasn't beside her, she panicked. She jumped up and ran downstairs. There, he sat at the kitchen table reading the paper and drinking coffee.

"Hey, hon, good morning, how's it going?" Will greeted her.

"I woke up in a panic, thought you took off," Deedee said.

"Took off," he said to her. "Just kidding. Want me to make you a cup of decaf tea?"

"No, I can do it. Thank you," she said. "You relax and drink your coffee."

There was a pitter patter of little feet, down the stairs came Trey Allan Wilson, flying into the kitchen, jumping in his mother's lap.

Will said, "Hey, hey kiddo! Take it easy on mommy."

"What's wrong with mommy?" Trey asked as he climbed down from her lap. He now was way too big to jump on anyone's lap. Trey was seven but he was tall and thick. He hung his head, walking away.

"I am sorry, mommy," he said. Trey still had not been told about the twins, that he was going to be a big brother.

"It's okay bab,y. Mommy is fine."

Trey sat at the table and DeeDee got his breakfast.

"Do you want oatmeal and eggs this morning?" asked DeeDee.

"Yuck, mommy," he cried, looking at her. "No, I hate oatmeal and eggs too. Trey didn't remember that he had eaten them in the hospital. He scarfed them down back then.

"Okay honey, it's cereal then," DeeDee declared. He ate one bowl but asked for another. He ate that as well.

"We are going to the movies but first we will go to the kid's museum," DeeDee announced. Trey was so happy and so was DeeDee.

"Okay, let's clean up the dishes and get out of here," Will told his crew. They left via the garage, but when they drove from the back to the front, Will noticed that the car was gone. Just a visitor, he thought. He headed south onto the highway.

"This is a good day," he told his wife.

"A very good day," she echoed. They talked about when they should tell Trey about the twins.

"He is doing so well. How would he take it? Would he be happy, would he be sad, would he, would he?" DeeDee asked.

But the consensus was not to tell him until she began to show more. DeeDee had an appointment on Tuesday at 1 p.m. Will would take her on his lunch break. They should be back before it was time for Carmen to leave, since she had to pick her daughter up from school.

Nurse Carmen arrived early; she was excited to start her new job. She was excited to get to know the Wilsons, especially Trey. He appeared to have gone through so much. She had read the report from the agency. It was policy, they had to know what they were getting into, they would make the decision whether to accept the job or not. After reading, Carmen felt it was a challenge, she couldn't wait to begin.

She rang the doorbell and DeeDee answered.

"Good morning," she greeted Carmen. "Please come in."

"Thank you, DeeDee. I am ready to get started."

"Alright, then let's do this," said DeeDee. "I will be home schooling Trey. I will need you to give him his meds. He takes them three times daily. If he should have an episode, come I will show you in the kitchen where is sedative is. It's a syringe. I only need to show you where it is. You know what to do from there."

"I don't expect anything to happen, things have been going well for the last several days, the transition has gone very smoothly so far. I pray it remains like that. I really need you to be here, to assist me if need be. You can do whatever you like. Did you bring any reading material?"

"No, but I did bring my computer," said Carmen.

"You are welcome to join us for lunch. Trey gets his break at noon," offered DeeDee.

"Yes, thank you. I would like to join you both, it will give me a chance to get a feel for Trey," the nurse suggested. "I want to know how he'll take to me. Do you think that I could maybe get a few minutes alone with him before I leave for the day?"

"Absolutely!" DeeDee was liking her already.

It was Tuesday morning, Carmen had arrived, she was just in time for breakfast and coffee. Will was pleased to see Carmen again since he had already left when she got there yesterday. They sat and had coffee. When it was time for Will to leave for work, he said his goodbyes, gave hugs and kisses and left.

"I will see you at 12:30 p.m., honey," he said before leaving.

Today was DeeDee appointment for her twelve-week checkup and so they could find out the sex of their twins. Carmen got along famously with Trey yesterday, but today they would spend a couple of hours alone together. DeeDee was apprehensive, because she had never left Trey alone with anyone before. She prayred and gave it to God.

DeeDee left for her appointment, giving Carmen instructions. Carmen asked if she could continue the home schooling from the morning.

"Yes, of course, you can, that will be very helpful," DeeDee agreed. "Thank you, Carmen."

"You be a good boy, Trey," she said to Trey.

"I am always a good boy, mommy," Trey answered. DeeDee left.

They were excited to be back in the doctor's office. The nurse called DeeDee and Will immediately. Dr. Maas entered the exam room. DeeDee was ready and anxiously waiting for the doctor. Dr. Maas asked DeeDee to lie back and relax. She began the sonogram. There were the two heartbeats again. Loud and clear. Two, not one, but two living beings growing inside DeeDee's tummy.

"Do you want to know what the twins' sexes are?" the doctor asked.

"Yes," DeeDee beamed with anticipation.

"Look here," she told them. "There is one penis and then another penis. They are boys, you are having twin boys!"

Will hugged his wife as if never letting her go. They both cried right there in the exam room. Dr. Maas told them she would give them space and that she'd be back in a few minutes.

The Wilson's collected themselves, thanked the doctor, and left for home. They had made the decision to tell Trey after dinner. Will would drop DeeDee back at home and head back to work.

DeeDee went into the house where things were eerily quiet. She went into the office and found Trey was sitting at his desk, with Carmen beside him watching him do his math. They never heard DeeDee enter the room. Carmen looked up to see DeeDee standing there quietly watching. DeeDee put her finger to her lips and backed out of the room.

She went into the kitchen to make a cup of tea. DeeDee thought she would allow Carmen to finish up with Trey for the day. Carmen still had an hour or so before her shift was over. DeeDee sat at the kitchen table, reminiscing about the day's good news. She rubbed her stomach and thanked the good Lord for not just the twins, but all the blessings that he always bestowed upon her family. She was more than grateful to have Trey home and doing well. She hoped that he would continue to thrive. DeeDee said softly, "Lord, your will be done. Let us accept your will no matter what."

Carmen went into the kitchen when she and Trey were finished, Trey in tow.

"Mommy, I didn't know you were home," Trey said to his mother.

"I am going to head out now," Carmen told DeeDee. "I will see you tomorrow morning bright and early."

"Yes, dear be safe," she said. "Thank you for continuing with Trey's studies.

"It was my pleasure. We got along well."

After Carmen was gone, Trey told his mother that he liked Nurse Carmen. What a relief, DeeDee thought.

"You can go to your room and play until dinner is ready," she told her child. Trey went to his room.

It was close to four o'clock when DeeDee took her pork chops out of the fridge to marinate them for dinner. She thought she heard something coming from the basement, their rec room. She dared not enter to check it out alone. She locked the door until Will got home. She checked to make sure the house was secure. It was like a fortress; it was almost next to impossible for anyone to get past all the security. She wouldn't take any chances. She went back to preparing her meal. Will would be home soon.

When Will arrived home, she heard the alarm. She was relieved, remembering the noise she thought she heard coming from the basement. Her husband walked into the kitchen, and she threw her arms around her husband's neck.

He hugged her, "what's going on?"

"I'm so glad you are home," DeeDee said.

"How's Trey?"

Oh, he's doing fine. Though I thought I heard a noise coming from the basement. I didn't go down; I locked the door."

"I'll check it out, honey. Settle down," Will assured her. "This house is tighter than a drum."

Will wasn't taking any chances. He went to the lock box to retrieve his weapon before entering the basement. Then, Will yelled from downstairs. "All is well, honey, probably just the house still settling."

Will went to the front window to check on the car across the street. It was back in the same spot.

DeeDee called Trey to come help set the table, and to tell him that his father is home. Trey gave his dad a big hug.

"How was your day?" he asked his son.

"It was great, Dad. I like Nurse Carmen, she is very nice, she helped me with my schoolwork, too."

"Great buddy! We have some good news for you later. After dinner."

"Okay, dad!" Trey acknowledged his father. He then went to set the table. He really enjoyed helping his mom.

Not a lot had changed, things were pretty much back to the way they were five months ago and before the mass on the brain had been discovered.

When dinner was finished, Trey helped his mom just as he always had. Dessert was served in the living room. DeeDee brought out the tray tables and served strawberry short cake with vanilla ice cream.

"Yummy, yummy," Trey beamed. Will was happy too.

When the family finished eating, Trey and DeeDee cleared the tray tables and cleaned the kitchen. DeeDee and Trey went back to the living room to rejoin Will.

"Alright, come sit with me and mommy," Will said to Trey. He headed over to the sofa to sit between his mother and father. DeeDee put her arms around her son.

DeeDee spoke, "Honey, you are going to be a big brother. In about four months, we are having twin boys."

"We?" Trey shouted; he didn't understand.

"The family is going to have two new babies. They are twins," DeeDee explained.

Trey jumped from the sofa from between his parents and stood in the middle of the living room, ranting.

"I don't want to be a big brother. You, me, and daddy. That's all I want," he exclaimed. "No twins, mommy, no boys, and no girls!"

Then he ran to his room in a huff, determined that he was not at all happy with the news.

DeeDee was flabbergasted, Will was in total shock. "Now what?" he asked his wife.

"I don't know what. I think he will be okay once he gets used to the idea," DeeDee was sure.

"I sure hope so. I can't take his outbursts again.

I truly believe, and I am praying that this too shall pass. I am going to give it to God," she told her husband reassuringly.

It was getting late, DeeDee went up to get Trey ready for bed. Will came up later. Trey was sitting on the side of his bed, unreceptive to his mom's arrival.

"Mommy, why do we have to have boys? I like it with you and daddy."

"You will be fine once they are here, and you can hold them," said DeeDee. "You are going to be a wonderful big brother. You wait and see."

"No mommy, no! Go away," he told her. "I want to go to sleep."

"But don't you want your story before you say goodnight?"

"No! I will say my prayers and go to sleep. Please go away."

DeeDee covered him with his blanket, turned out his light, closed his door and left. Will has already had a shower. He was in bed; he was at Trey's door and heard the conversation. He didn't bother him.

"He must be better in the morning. We want him to be a part of the entire pregnancy," DeeDee said.

"We need our son," Will told DeeDee.

"I know, honey, I know." They slept. They slept.

Tomorrow was a new day. Will was the first to rise, DeeDee in his wake. She went down to start breakfast while Will showered and got ready for work. Not a peep yet from Trey. Will entered the kitchen and had coffee only.

"Honey, are you going to be alright today?" he asked.

"I will be fine," DeeDee answered. "Carmen will arrive soon."

"I am going to go in early so that I can come home early," Will said and collected his work gear and headed to work.

Carmen arrived soon after Will left the house.

"Good morning," DeeDee let her in. She told Carmen of the occurrences of the last night. Carmen did not say a word, but she thought it was far too early to bring Trey into baby news. He was still too fragile, in her opinion as a professional.

"Did you talk to his doctor about the opportune time to break the news to him?" Carmen asked.

"Well, no we didn't. We considered our own instincts," said DeeDee. "Why? Do you have some thoughts on when he should have been told?"

Nurse Carmen stayed in her place and took the easy way out. She declined to discuss it further. DeeDee gave Carmen coffee, and she went about her way. Still nothing from Trey. DeeDee went to check on her son. He was still asleep. She let him sleep for another thirty minutes. He had to have breakfast and start his first session of home schooling.

DeeDee asked Carmen if she would start Trey off after he had his breakfast.

"Of course, I will," Carmen answered. "No worries."

"He likes you, he told us yesterday," DeeDee shared.

"I like him also, he's a sweet kid."

"I have some chores to finish. Thank you," DeeDee said. "I will get him up shortly."

"That's fine, I will be in the office waiting for him." DeeDee got Trey washed up and down for his breakfast. He ate in silence, not even looking at his mother.

"Nurse Carmen is at your desk waiting for you to help you with your schoolwork today," Trey perked right up.

"I don't want to eat," he said. "I want to go do my work."

"You need to sit and eat your breakfast. After which you can go to your desk," DeeDee said firmly.

Trey wasn't pleased, but he did as he was told. Trey scarfed down his cereal, drank his juice, cleared his bowl to the sink, and ran to see Nurse Carmen.

DeeDee went about her chores. She was not bothered because she knew that Trey was in good hands. Will called to check on his family, DeeDee told him all was well. Trey is in the office with Nurse Carmen, she is working with Trey on the first session today, and I am getting some chores out of the way.

"Okay, honey. I will be home early. See you later." The conversation ended.

DeeDee prepared lunch for all three of them. "Lunch is ready for you two," she called out to them both, when it was ready.

When lunch was over DeeDee cleared and cleaned the dishes. Carmen and Trey returned to the office.

Time had gone by quickly; it was almost time for Carmen to leave for the day. DeeDee had gotten quite a bit done. She went to the office to let Carmen know that she could leave. Trey didn't want her to go. He was starting to act out, not terribly but he wasn't happy that she was leaving.

"I will be back in the morning, honey. Please be a good boy," Carmen soothed the child. DeeDee's feelings were hurt. She had issues with the fact that Trey didn't want Carmen to leave.

"Come on, honey. She will be back in the morning," she pulled Trey to her, and Carmen left. Trey retreated to his room.

Here we go again, DeeDee thought.

Rita Collins has been stalking the Wilson house for days. She wants their son. She is just waiting for the right time. Shelia, also known as Rita Collins, has suffered from mental instability most of her adult life. She has done well to mask it. Rita has been subscribed to a cocktail of four different medications. How she kept herself under the radar is a mystery. Her pseudonym is about to be revealed. The FBI is on her heels. It's only a matter of time.

Rita Collins, refuses, or rather cannot let go of the incident with Trey. She thought he needed to learn a lesson because he humiliated her. She often agonized over it. Rita Collins wouldn't rest until she got revenge. Who in their right mind would want to hurt a child?

Will arrived home and DeeDee was in the kitchen.

"Dinner is almost done," she yelled.

Will was somewhat out of sorts, the car still sat across the street. It was there when he left for work, and it still sits there, only now there was someone occupying the left back passenger seat. Will couldn't make out whether it was a man or woman, but he didn't like it. He dared not tell his wife. He didn't want to upset her. He left the front window, went to the kitchen to greet DeeDee.

"Hi, honey! How was your day?"

"It was okay, I guess," DeeDee answered.

"You guess? What happened?"

"Trey was trying to act out," said DeeDee. "He didn't want Carmen to leave, and he was sullen after she did. He went to his room; I haven't seen him since. I went upstairs unannounced and peeked in on him. He was watching TV."

"So, I let him be. I was almost afraid to say anything to him. It isn't right, Will," DeeDee continued. "I should not be afraid of my own son."

"He was gone for five months, honey," Will said. "It will take some time for all of us to re-acclimate ourselves to each other."

DeeDee shook her head in agreement.

Trey came down when he heard his father's voice.

"Hi, daddy!" He gave his father a weak hug, nothing like the usual bear hug.

"How was your day, buddy?" Will asked his son.

"It was okay, I guess," Trey said.

"Now, you are guessing?" Will chimed. Trey didn't understand what his father was referring to.

Trey sat at the table, DeeDee looked his way with her hand on her hip. "Please set the table, Trey. What are you waiting for?"

Trey wasn't responding to DeeDee's liking.

"Get a move on, child!" DeeDee said again. "What's going on with you?"

He slammed the plates down on the table. Will put his hand on his son's shoulder. "Are you okay?" Will asked Trey.

"Daddy, I don't want to be a big brother," he said. "I want you, me, and mommy."

"We can't make them go away, and besides you will love your brothers once they are here," explained Will. Trey was not getting it, and apparently his parents weren't getting it either. They were not listening.

"Okay," he told his dad, still not addressing his mother, not acknowledging his mother.

He sat at the table never once looking up. It was a very quiet dinner. After dinner, Trey asked his father if he could go to his room, since he didn't feel well. DeeDee agreed since she would rather Trey go to his room than be around her with his attitude. The best thing was he was still under control. No major outbursts. Thank God!

Time had flown by. DeeDee's tummy was growing at a rapid pace. After all she was toting around two babies. There will be two new additions to the Wilson family soon. Carmen had been a lifesaver; she was schooling Trey daily now. DeeDee had prepared several frozen meals to make it easier for her. She didn't have to cook every day; she now took meals from the freezer. It would also be easier for the boys when she went into labor.

Liz would take over the chores and meals while DeeDee was recuperating. Trey had been on his best behavior over the last months. He enjoyed having Carmen around. He also liked that she was home schooling him. DeeDee wasn't particular about not being close to him, but it worked.

She was due any day now, so Will had taken leave from work. Carmen and Liz were there most of the time now. Liz was starting to stay over, to be with Trey when DeeDee and Will had to leave to go to the hospital.

It was 2 a.m. when DeeDee's water broke. Her bags were packed, she was ready; but Will was a total panic. He kept telling her to breathe. He ran downstairs, leaving his wife, but then he remembered he had to help her.

Will went back to retrieve her and her bag. After helping her down to the front door, he woke Liz in a panic, it's time he told his sister-in-law.

Locking the door, he said to Liz, "I will arm the house from the car. We will call later."

The Wilsons were in the labor and delivery room for an hour before Travis arrived, two minutes later Trevor arrived. Will cut both cords. He laid his boys on their mommy's chest. Will laid with them. There laid two perfectly identical twin boys. Trevor had a mole over his left ear, otherwise you couldn't tell them apart. Travis weighed in at five pounds and seven ounces while Trevor weighed in at five pounds and four ounces. They were both nineteen inches long. DeeDee was exhausted, so was Will. He was as tired as if he had done the work. The nurse took the twins to be cleaned up.

"Please don't keep them too long," DeeDee told the nurse.

Dr. Maas stood on the bed beside the two of them and congratulated them again. DeeDee and Will would go to her room shortly; and her babies would join them later. DeeDee only needed to stay in the hospital for two days. That was long enough for her.

Rita Collins watched the entire event taking place out in front of the Wilson home. She saw when they left, she would wait for the opportune time to ring the doorbell.

It was 7:30 a.m. when the doorbell rang, followed by an immediate knock. Liz jumped up from the couch, she always slept on the sofa to be close to the door. She had a phobia about not being close to an exit. She gathered herself and went to the door.

"Who is it?" she asked.

"Good morning, my name is Rita, Rita Collins," answered the person on the other side of the door. Liz knew exactly who Rita Collins was.

"Get away from the door or I will call the police!"

Rita banged on the door with vengeance. She was pissed, but she left. Liz called the police. When the police arrived, they took a report and left. Trey never heard a thing.

Back at the hospital, the twins had been cleaned, checked out, and returned to their mommy and daddy. The boys were in perfect health. DeeDee could go home the next day. The nursery had been ready for months. Prayerfully Trey would be fine with the twins next door to his room. Will and DeeDee would soon find out his reaction to his new brothers.

Liz was now wide awake, and Trey had begun to stir. It was a beautiful, nice, and crisp Saturday morning in Marc. The sun was out in full force. Liz called Trey, he was up and getting washed up. There was no home schooling today, Carmen was scheduled to come to the house tomorrow, Sunday, to help DeeDee get acclimated, and settle in with the twins. Liz was staying over until Sunday evening. Everyone was set and in place. It was exciting. Trey and Liz had breakfast and hung out for the rest of the day. Liz didn't bring up the twins. The thought of Rita Collins lingered in Liz's mind all day long.

"What on earth was that woman up to?" Liz found herself speaking out loud. Will and DeeDee arrived home on Sunday, around 2 p.m. Carmen had already arrived. Her daughter wanted to come with her. But Carmen thought it would be too much, so Shanna stayed with her aunt for the day. Trey was in his room when his parents arrived. He hadn't heard or seen his brothers yet. Carmen and Liz helped DeeDee settle the twins in their cribs. It was a beautiful sight to see those two perfect little boys.

"How do you tell them apart?" Carmen asked DeeDee. DeeDee pointed to the mole above Trevor's ear.

"I am sure there will be other ways to tell them apart as they get older, of course," Carmen responded.

DeeDee took a chair in the room with the boys. She was breastfeeding for a few months. She didn't like it when Trey was born. But it's a new day and a new time, so she thought she would give it another try.

"We can keep an eye on the babies if you want to go lie down," Will said to his wife while rubbing her back.

"No, honey, I'm good, I want to be here when Trey meets his brothers for the first time."

Liz got Will's attention and motioned to him with a nod to follow her out of the room. The two went down to the kitchen, the farthest away. Liz didn't want to take any chances. This wasn't to be heard by all ears. Will gave Liz a quizzical look.

"What's up?" he asked.

That Rita Collins knocked on the door just hours after you took DeeDee to the hospital. She was very upset when I told her to leave. I told her to leave, or I would call the police," Liz told Will.

"Did you call the cops?" Will asked.

"Of course, I did, immediately," Liz replied.

"I don't want DeeDee to know, I don't want her upset," Will said. "She once thought she heard noises in the basement some time ago. I looked but nothing. I will call the FBI agent as well."

DeeDee called Will, and both Liz and Will went back up to the nursery. DeeDee wanted to have Trey meet his brothers. Will went into Trey's room.

"Come buddy," he called. "I have someone I want you to meet."

Trey didn't want to leave his room; however, reluctantly he obeyed his dad. Will led the way and once in the nursery, Will stepped aside for Trey to get a clear view of the cribs. Trey walked over to the cribs, one and then the other.

He turned around with a throaty, raspy unrecognizable voice. "I told you I did not want those boys to come here. Take them back to the hospital, now!" Trey screamed.

"Take him out, Will, before he wakes the babies," DeeDee said to her husband. Tears rolled down her cheeks, Liz went over to her and gave her a hug.

"It will be okay, sis. He must get used to the idea," Liz consoled her.

He has had months to get used to the idea. What are we going to do if he doesn't get used to the idea?"

"Give him a little time," Carmen tried to reassure her. "Once he sees that they are a part of the family, he will come around." This is the very first time in months that DeeDee felt uneasy about Trey being home. He had his moments.

"Did you hear how his voice changed?" she recalled. It was unsettling, she thought. Everyone else agreed. They didn't voice their opinions out loud.

Trey stayed in his room the rest of the day until dinnertime. Liz took meals from the oven to place them in the microwave. She had Trey come down and set the table. But he didn't speak quietly when about his way. He took his time, but he did it. There would four places, because Carmen was staying for dinner. Liz went home after all the dishes had been done. Carmen would also be going home. Will had taken FMLA. Carmen was scheduled to return early on Monday morning.

If Trey didn't want any part of his brothers, DeeDee was fine with that. Will called the FBI agent and left a message on his voicemail concerning the visit from Rita. DeeDee missed Trey's presence, but she did not like his new attitude. He began to act out again, though not as severe as in the past. But acting out at all was too much for her, especially with the babies now home.

Agent Thompson returned Will's call early Monday morning, Will relayed what had taken place. Will gave a description of the car that sat across the street. They finished the conversation, and he went to check on his three son three and his wife. Carmen was making breakfast, and DeeDee was feeding the boys. Trey had not surfaced from his room.

Will knocked on Trey's door, then he entered. "Hey buddy! what's up?" he asked his son.

"I don't like those boys and I don't want them here," said Trey. Will went over to Treyand patted a spot in his bed for Trey to come sit. He went over to join his father.

Will placed his arm around his son and proceeded to explain. Trey sat for a few minutes, then jumped from the bed.

"I do not want those boys in this house!" Trey was adamant.

Will stood up and walked to the door, "Breakfast will be ready shortly, wash up, and come down to join your family."As far as the matter of your brothers is concerned, they are not going anywhere. You are almost nine years old. There is no reason for your behavior. Your medications are working and have been for quite a while. I expect you to behave yourself."

Will left the room and closed the door.

Trey kicked his TV; it didn't break but as hard as he kicked it should have. Will heard the commotion; however, he opted to let him be.

I know this is a major adjustment for him, I am trying my best to be patient with my son, I will continue to work with him, so his adjustment won't be so difficult, Will thought this to himself as he went down to watch the news and wait for breakfast.

DeeDee refused to leave the babies alone. Will brought her breakfast up to her. She was no longer breastfeeding, so she was pumping her milk and freezing it for the twins. It had only been a few days, but for some reason she didn't like it, feeling like it was not for her.

When breakfast was done, Will and Trey cleared, cleaned, and put the dishes away. Carmen was in the office preparing to homeschool Trey. Trey was pleased that he would be spending some time alone with Carmen. She was his friend. At least that's how he thought of her. He had decided that he didn't like his mom or dad. Especially don't like those boys. He had decided that he would get rid of them by any means necessary. Trey would be nine on his birthday. Not only was he big, strong, and tall for his age, but he was also very smart and very cunning. He was thinking some wicked thoughts.

Time went by fast, the twins grew and became more and more alert. Trey had warmed to them a little. He still was opposed to having much interaction with them. He went into the nursery to see his mother from time to time, only staring at his brothers. DeeDee always asked him if he wanted to hold them, he always declined, afraid that he might break them. DeeDee and Will laughed and shrugged it off. Carmen took him more seriously. God only knew what going on in his head.

Three months had passed, it was time for Will to return to work. DeeDee hated the fact that he had to leave.

"Someone had to earn a paycheck," he always said to her, when it got closer for him to go back to work.

Carmen worked long hours and sometimes she'd bring her daughter with her, they'd stay the night on occasion. Shanna had been at school early, Carmen took her to school and returned directly, making it back before Trey awoke.

Trevor and Travis, awfully cute, were identical down to the point it was hard for strangers to tell them apart. They both weighed in at five pounds and five ounces and were twenty-three inches long. It's almost like they were challenging each other to see who would grow the fastest. DeeDee was adding cereal to their milk.

She still had a hard time convincing Trey to play with his brothers. Although he made up his mind to pick them up a couple of times. Didn't hold them long, never close to his body, Trey held his brothers out like they had pooped or something. He quickly gave them back.

Trey thought to himself, I wish you two would go away.

His father asked him once did he know which baby was which. He responded no and that he really doesn't care.

"I like them now," Trey expounded. "But I don't care what their names are." Will shook his head, DeeDee prayed.

Will and DeeDee had talked of maybe, in the future, when the twins were six months old, DeeDee could return to teaching part-time. Carmen seemed to be doing a fantastic job helping with everything. There was also talk of Carmen and Shanna taking the rec room in the basement. It could be converted into a small one-bedroom apartment for the two of them. Will was happy to convert it. Carmen was at their house so much, she already felt that she lived there. She was happy with her job; Shanna was happy too. She and Trey got along well. She would love to move to the Wilson's home. It would be a wonderful place to live. Besides, she loved those two little boys. Shanna would be old enough to babysit for the Wilson's son too.

Will spent his weekends converting the basement, Carmen's lease ended in a month. Will promised to have the basement ready before then. DeeDee hadn't been down to the basement in months. Will asked her to come see it, and when DeeDee went down to the basement, she was shocked. She didn't know her husband had it in him. It was so pretty and perfect for Carmen and Shanna. They would be pleased. Will refused to let them see it before he was done.

When Carmen and Shanna were allowed to see their new home, Will led them down to the basement. They were both told to place their hands over their eyes. When they took the last step, they opened their eyes, and Carmen let out a gasp. Shanna was jumping around. They loved it and couldn't wait to move in. DeeDee missed the hoopla as she was with the twins.

Trey wasn't impressed. He was pleased that they were moving in but the place itself was no big deal. Nothing was a big deal to Trey. His interest waned in comparison to other boys his age. Carmen and Shanna had moved in; it was now a one big happy family.

The twins were about to turn six months old, and Trey was about to be nine years old. Carmen had agreed to sit with the twins, DeeDee had an appointment for a reinstatement class. It had been years since she had been in a classroom. She kept up her certification just in case. She had always hoped that one day she would be able to teach another class of fifth graders. Even if it was a few days a week.

It was a rainy day on the first of September, Carmen knew the routine. Shanna was at school. Trey had his breakfast and was in his room. DeeDee left looking great and feeling great. She told Carmen she should be home in a couple of hours.

"We will be fine," Carmen said to DeeDee. "Knock 'em dead."

Carmen checked on the twins and called Trey to come for his morning session. The twins were in their playpen, the boys were sitting up already. Trey came down to the office and sat at his desk. He appeared to be distant. He wasn't himself. He had something on his mind but only God knew what. Carmen had become a woman of faith as DeeDee had won her over. She said a prayer before she started his lesson.

Their first session soon ended. After which, Carmen fed the twins, then put them down for a nap. She went to the kitchen to make lunch. When it was ready, she called Trey, but he didn't answer. She called again, still no answer. Carmen went to look for him.

Trey was hiding at the top of the stairs. Carmen reached the top of the stairs and that's all she remembers. Trey hit her with his baseball bat. She woke later, she struggled to gather herself, she was on the floor in the hallway upstairs.

She finally came to herself to remember being hit with something. Carmen called out to Trey, no answer. Trey was not in the house.

Carmen immediately ran to check on the twins, and upon entering the nursery, she fell to the floor and screamed. "Nooooooooo!!!!"

Both boys were on the floor outside of the playpen. They were blue. Carmen felt for a pulse but there was no pulse. She went to get her cell phone and called 911.

Carmen was so hysterical she could barely speak. When she was finally able to get out that she thought the babies were dead, she fainted. The banging on the front door and the doorbell ringing incessantly brought her back to the world of the living. She ran to the door. The fire department was standing with the crash axe, ready to break the door down.

The EMT's asked her where the children were. She took them to the nursery. Trevor, and Travis laid on the floor, not moving. Each EMT both took a child and started working on them. Their efforts were fruitless. The children had expired. Carmen was in shock.

"Is there anyone else in the house, ma'am?" another EMT asked.

"No sir. Just me," Carmen answered. "I was sitting for the children," Carmen stopped. "The oldest boy, Trey, is missing. He had to do this. I was hit with something, and I was out for a bit. Don't know exactly how long but But when I came to, I saw the babies and Trey was nowhere to be found."

"Are you the parent?" By this time, the police had arrived. There must have been ten people in the house.

Carmen answered the police officer. "No, I am not the parent. How will I tell their parents?"

"You need to call the parents; the medical examiner is on the way," the officer advised.

Carmen was in a state of denial. She did not, could not, believe that those beautiful babies were dead.

She called Will first and he promptly answered. "Hey Carmen, is everything alright?"

"No, Mr. Wilson. You need to come home," Carmen said.

Will thought to himself, why is Carmen calling me Mr. Wilson?

"Carmen, what's wrong?" he asked.

"It's the babies, Mr. Wilson. Something has happened to the babies," Carmen cried. Before Will could ask another question, the phone went dead.

The medical examiner was with the twins.

"It looks like suffocation," he said aloud, shaking his head. "I will know more after the autopsies. Who would do such a terrible thing? These children didn't stand a chance."

Will pulled up in his driveway. There were police cars, policemen, fire trucks, firemen, and an ambulance. Things didn't sink in until he saw the medical examiner's truck.

"Oh god, let me by, I live here," he said upon entering. "Where are my boys?"

A police officer tried to stop him but let him through. Carmen was standing in the living room sobbing uncontrollably.

"Where is Trey?" he asked. She couldn't say a word, she only shrugged her shoulders. She didn't know.

Will ran upstairs into the nursery. There were two white sheets covering his babies. Will broke down, he crawled over to where they lay side by side. Will pulled the sheets off and his boys' lips were blue. They looked like they were sleeping, except for the color. He fell over them and wailed. William Wilson was in agony, he was broken.

He felt a hand pull him away from them and pull him up from the floor.

"Please, Mr. Wilson. I am sorry for your loss," said one of the police officers. "But let's make it easier for the medical examiner to do his job." They put his babies in a little black tarp, each in his own bag, and carried them out.

Detective Singleton had arrived, DeeDee unaware of what had taken places. He had not arrived back home yet. Will collected himself enough to think not to call his wife for fear that she may have an accident or something worse. Will sat down with Detective Singleton to ask some questions. He needed to get some clarity.

"First, I would like to say I am so sorry for your loss," the detective said.

Will thanked him, and between sobs, "how am I going to tell my wife?"

"I know that this is hard for you, but we must find out what happened here," the detective continued. "I understand you have an older son?"

"Yes, Trey, he's almost nine."

"Do you have any idea where he might be?"

"He's only nine, he doesn't know a whole lot of people. I have no idea, Detective."

"I will go to talk to your housekeeper."

"She's our home care nurse. She lives with us."

Detective Singleton found Carmen sitting in the kitchen still sobbing. He sat down at the table with his pad and pen in hand. He introduced himself, and asked Carmen for her name.

"My name is Carmen," she answered.

"Carmen, so you found the boys?"

"I found them when I woke up."

"You were asleep?"

"I went to look for the oldest child and when I reached the top of the stairs, I was struck by something," Carmen narrated. "When I awoke, I found the babies and the older boy was gone. I called for him several times, his backpack was gone and the clothes that he was wearing were on the floor in his room. I called 911 before I went looking for Trey."

"He's had some mental issues, but he was doing well, or so we thought. I can't even fathom how Mrs. Wilson will take this," she started to cry harder, her body was shaking with grief. "Is there anything else, Detective"

"No, that's all for now."

The Detective went back to talk to Will, he handed him his card.

"If you hear from your son, or you think of anything else, give me a call. I will be in touch." he said and left.

The detective cleared everybody out. Will asked the detective if they could remove the crime scene tape. "I want my wife to come inside before she knows anything is wrong."

"Yes, I will have the officer remove it," the detective agreed.

Will sat in the nursery by himself. *I don't know how to tell my wife. God, please help me,* Will started to pray. *I am asking for strength, God; I am asking for you to give us the strength to get through this travesty. Two of my sons are deceased and I don't know where the other one could be. How do I tell my wife? I know you don't hear from me often, but I am reaching out to you now, please hear my prayer.* Will sat on the floor and waited for his wife to return home.

Carmen pulled herself together enough to go pick Shanna up from school. She was getting her early. She didn't want to be home when Mrs. Wilson arrived. They needed to be alone. She somehow felt responsible.

"Things were going so well," she spoke out loud.

"What was going on? Why are you getting me from school early and why have you been crying? What's wrong mom?" Shanna asked her mom.

Carmen didn't answer, just tears streaming down her face. They headed back home, went straight to the basement. Then, she would tell Shanna what happened.

Trey was on the run again. This time, it was thought that he knew what he was doing. He was with Rita Collins. Rita had somehow managed to get him to come with her. She saw him on a park bench. Rita asked him why he was out there alone. He told her that he ran away. When she asked him why, he said that he did not like those boys.

Rita knew of the twins, but she had no idea that Trey wasn't happy with them. Why would she, she was out of the loop. Rita was on the run as well.

"Get in," she told Trey. "You can go to my house, no one will be able to find you there."

He got in gladly to get off the street. For some strange reason, Trey didn't remember her. Rita had been lying in wait for the right time to nab Trey. She now had her chance for revenge on this kid that humiliated her almost a year ago. Rita was on the path to her fate as well. Rita lived across town in a condo. She had been there for four years, living under the radar and eluding the FBI. She was a heartless criminal, waiting, watching, following the Wilson boy. No one is wiser.

Trey was reluctant to leave her car, but after a few minutes he went with her.

"What do you like to eat?" she asked him as she was unlocking the front door.

"Peanut butter and jelly," answered Trey.

Peanut Butter and jelly it is then!

When Rita went to take his backpack, Trey jerked away.

"No!" Trey exclaimed. Rita backed off. He refused to remove it, sat at the table in her dining room, ate his sandwich, and drank his milk in silence. Trey was starving. When he was finished, he asked to use the bathroom. Rita showed him where it was.

Trey was carrying his dad's .45 gun in his backpack; he had taken it after smothering his brothers. Will had mistakenly forgotten to lock his lockbox. He had removed it to check the basement months ago. Trey returned to the dining room where Rita was bending down at a cabinet. Trey took the door stop he found near the bathroom and clunked Rita over the head, with such force it knocked her out cold, just as he had done to Carmen earlier that morning. He stood over her staring down at her body. He took the weapon from his backpack and fired two shots at Rita Collins. One in the face and another in her chest right above her heart. Trey left by way of a rear window. He was gone again.

DeeDee arrived home and the house had a somber feel. She didn't see or hear anyone. She called out to her husband. No answer. She called out to Carmen. She went up to the nursery and there Will sat on the floor by the cribs holding a teddy bear.

DeeDee looked in the cribs. "Where are my children?" she asked, not yet feeling anything to be wrong.

Will stood up and embraced his wife. "Honey, the boys are gone."

"Gone where?"

"They are dead, honey," Will revealed. "Our babies are dead, and Trey is missing."

He struggled to hold her up, but she had passed out. Will placed her on the floor. He laid there holding her, trying to bring her back. When he finally succeeded, she screamed at the top of her lungs. Will cried as he held his wife, he didn't try to console her because there was no consolation. They sat there on the floor holding each other, sobbing for what seemed like hours.

When DeeDee spoke, she asked, "Will, what happened?"

"From what we know, Trey suffocated his brothers."

"Oh my God!" She was sobbing uncontrollably and so was Will. It was hard for him but even harder to see his wife in so much pain. He had time to process the God-awful tragedy, but DeeDee was just now having to deal with it.

"Where is Trey?" she asked.

"I don't know. He hit Carmen over the head, murdered the twins, and took off."

Trey's face was all over the news and an APB had been sent out.

"Police all over the city are looking for our son. Murderer. Can this be true? Did he plan this? Is he that evil after all?" DeeDee asked her husband.

"My babies, my babies," she cried, and cried for her babies, all three of them.

Will gave DeeDee a sedative to relax her a bit and to numb the pain. Nothing would take the pain away, he thought, but he needed his wife. He had lost his children, he wasn't going to lose his wife too.

Will carried his wife to their bedroom. DeeDee tried to resist him, she wanted to stay near her boys. He managed to get her undressed and lying down as the medication had started to take effect. Will sat on the side of the bed beside his wife and cried some more.

"I cannot believe this is happening," he was thinking out loud.

Carmen was in her little place in the basement with Shanna. She had not gone into detail concerning the tragedies of the day, she only disclosed that Trey had gone missing. Shanna had no idea the twins were dead. Carmen thought it best not to upset her with that awful news. She would find out soon enough.

Will went to the living room to turn on the news, and there, as large as life, was his oldest child being labeled a murderer. The coroner's report would take a few days. Will was in a state of disbelief. Carmen walked into the living room and sat down on the sofa. Her eyes were puffy as were Will's.

"I am so sorry, Mr. Wilson," she said.

"Please don't call me Mr. Wilson. We are family," Will tried to console here. "This is not your fault, Carmen."

"I feel like I am somehow responsible for what happened," Carmen told Will.

"No one could have known. No one," said Will. "Trey seemed to be warming to the twins. If he did this, and everything is pointing to him, then I believe this was his plan all along." They sat in silence for a moment, then Carmen asked where DeeDee was.

"I gave her a sedative. Her doctor prescribed a light dosage for her when Trey was in the hospital," he told her. "She's resting, you might want to go up and check on her please, see if she needs anything."

Rita's neighbor, Lisa, heard a loud bang coming from Rita's condo. She went to the front door and knocked, no answer. She then proceeded to the back patio and the side window was open. Lisa returned to her condo and rang the police. They were there in no time, sirens blazing, lights flashing. The officer knocked on the door too, still no answer. One officer stayed at the front and two officers went to the back of Rita's condo. The window screen had been kicked out of one of the windows. An officer climbed through the window.

On the dining room floor laid a woman, in a pool of blood, with two bullet wounds, one to her face and the other to body. The officer looked around and called out.

"Is anyone here?" He opened the back door for his partner.

"Call it in. This woman is deceased."

Once again, a mass of people had surrounded another property. Only this time they were on the other side of town.

DeeDee had begun to stir when Carmen knocked on the door.

"Come in," DeeDee told her. Carmen ran over to the bed where DeeDee was sitting up and hugged her. The two women hugged and cried.

"My babies, my babies. I want to see my babies. All three. Where was Trey?" DeeDee cried.

Carmen went to get Will. DeeDee needed to talk to him. Will raced up the stairs to his wife.

DeeDee told Will she was going to get dressed. She was going to see her babies, at least two of them. Will tried to talk her out of it but DeeDee wasn't listening.

Thirty minutes later, Will and DeeDee were at the morgue, demanding to see the twins. The officer on duty called back to the medical examiner who agreed to send them down. The medical examiner had not started to perform the autopsy yet.

The two walked to the window and the twins were rolled up and uncovered.

DeeDee screamed and proceeded to bang savagely on the paned glass window.

"No, no, no!" She tried to get into the room with them, but the door was locked.

She looked at the medical examiner through the window. "Please let me hold my babies. Please," she begged.

The medical examiner went to the door to let them in. He felt the pain of this mother and father. He had to oblige them. They slowly went over to the table, DeeDee kissed Trevor, and then she kissed Travis, on their sweet little cheeks.

"Mommy is so sorry, daddy is so sorry," they told their boys.

They looked to be asleep. But they weren't, they were dead, and likely at the hands of their big brother. DeeDee put her arms around her boys one at a time and told them she loved them.

"Mommy will see you again one day," she told her boys.

They went back into the hallway; the curtains were closed. Their babies were out of sight.

DeeDee screamed. "My babies, my babies!" Her body went limp.

Will caught her before she hit the floor and he called for help. Someone brought a wheelchair. Will took his wife back to the empty place they called home. It wouldn't seem like much of a home without their children now.

Detective Singleton had arrived at the crime scene, where Rita's body had been discovered. Yellow crime tape had been placed all the way around from front to back. Forensics was dusting the place for prints. The detective was informed that the deceased was Rita Collins, using her purse on the counter in the kitchen. In it was her driver's license, credit cards, checks, as well as a revolver. The detective was aware of the name Rita Collins, which was her alias. She was on the FBI most wanted list.

"Well, here you are, Rita Collins, you have finally met your match," he said.

He would be shocked when he found out who that match was. The medical examiner arrived, did his preliminary evaluations, and had Rita's body bagged and taken to the truck. The same truck that housed two six-month-old baby boys only hours prior. The crime scene was wrapped up and everyone left.

Will and DeeDee had arrived back home, with DeeDee still seemed to be in a daze. She had dried her tears, she felt completely num. Carmen had made a little supper for the two of them. Shanna was sitting in the kitchen.

"They would find Trey soon," she said to the two of them.

"Yes, of course, we want to find Trey," Will said. "But in the meantime, we must prepare to lay our twins to rest."

Shanna looked to her mother, looked to the Wilson's as if to say what are you talking about. Carmen took her to the basement, to bring her up on what had happened. There was a blood curdling scream that arose from the apartment below. They were not aware Shanna had not been told.

Detective Singleton notified the FBI of the death of Rita Collins. The FBI would meet him at the station to obtain a copy of the report. The autopsy was to take place on the next morning, to confirm the official cause of death.

The phone rang. It was Liz, just checking on her family, she said when DeeDee answered the phone.

DeeDee handed Will the phone as she couldn't talk. Will told his sister-in-law what was going on and Liz dropped the phone. She did not return to the line. Twenty minutes later, the doorbell rang repeatedly. Will went to the door, looked through the peephole, saw it was Liz, and opened the door. Liz hurried over to her sister, both cried. Will cried too. Carmen was downstairs trying to console her child. Shanna was a total mess.

After the initial shock, Liz started asking questions no one had the answers to, at least not yet. There were assumptions being made but nothing concrete. Not until Trey was apprehended and the autopsy was complete. All anyone could do was wait. My babies, were all DeeDee kept saying. Will would give her another sedative before bed. Liz asked if she could stay over, and Will responded that she never needed to ask as she is their family and was always welcomed in their home. She gave him a hug and said thanks bruh.

The autopsies were complete, and the official cause of death was asphyxia. The boys had been smothered. There was saliva on the pillow that had been used to commit the crime, from both boys. There were also fingerprints on the pillow, but there was no match. When they found Trey, they would take his prints to compare them to the ones on the pillow that was used to smother the twins.

The autopsy would be performed on Rita Collin's body on Monday, it was now Friday evening. The days seemed to be growing longer for the Wilson family. They should have started to make the arrangements for their boys, but they couldn't seem to muster up the energy. Liz would do most of the leg work, along with Carmen's assistance. Liz called the funeral home and made an appointment with the undertaker. Liz called the florist. She did whatever she could to make life a little easier for her family. They were so grateful to have her and Carmen around. Shanna wasn't going back to school until after the funeral.

DeeDee and Will had chosen matching outfits that the boys had never worn. Trevor and Travis would be laid to rest, side by side in the same coffin. White coffins with sky blue linings, they were going to be dressed in all white. Liz would even put shoes and socks on her babies. All white roses, and two doves. It was a very sad time, but it had to be done. DeeDee was making a step forward, one foot at a time, one day at a time. Will was right there by his wife's side every step of the way.

One day, he thought to himself, you must be very careful what you put out into the universe. I remember when my son Trey was very mentally ill, I said I wanted him to be put away. I wanted my life before him, now my life will never be the same again. From the looks of things my oldest son is going to be put away. Will regretted every word.

An autopsy had been completed on Rita Collin's body; the cause of death was a gunshot wound to the heart. She bled out. If she had been found sooner, she may have been saved. That's why it's called fate. She was not a nice person, from what was discovered about her, and it was not a nice way that she died. Fate. There was no next of kin on record. She would be buried in Chickasaw Field where the degenerates are laid to rest. No tombstone, only a stick cross with a number. Fate!

The services would be held at St. Joseph Baptist Church. The wake was at ten a.m. followed by the service at eleven a,m. Everyone was asked to wear white. The services had been posted on social media, as well as various news stations around town. The church was packed, folks came from all over to pay their respects. The Wilson's circle of friends was very small, but this tragedy was all over the news for days. Trey still had not been found. No one knew if he was dead or alive. Will and DeeDee were laying their children to rest and were so concerned about the other one. The service was beautiful, DeeDee even managed to say a few words about her babies.

"They were only six months old, but they had developed a personality. They will be missed," DeeDee said through her tears. There was no repass. They wanted to go home and greave alone.

Trey was wandering the streets. He was dirty, he was hungry, he was alone. He sat on a bench outside of a park, nearly two miles from his home. Still carrying his backpack with a loaded gun inside.

Two teenagers passed by him sitting there alone, one said to the other, "That's the boy on the news, you know the one that is suspected of murdering his baby brothers."

"Oh yeah, it looks like him, but let's just get a policeman."

Trey was a big boy, and they didn't want to make a mistake. What if it wasn't him.

Two police officers walked over to the bench.

"Hello," one said to Trey, carefully approaching the boy.

"What is your name, son?" asked the other one.

"My name is Trey Allan Wilson. I live at 7856 Parson Street with my mom and dad. They had two boys, but they are gone now, I made them go away."

The officers tried to remove his backpack, but Trey fought to keep it. One officer held Trey while the other separated him from the backpack. He was a big boy, the reports said he was nine but that was impossible. They cuffed the child, put him in the backseat of the patrol car, and drove him to the station.

They couldn't question him until his parents were present. Will and DeeDee got the call, after only just putting two babies in the ground the day was taking a new turn. Trey was apprehended the same day his brothers were buried.

The Wilsons arrived at the police station, Trey had been read his rights and processed, in the presence of a CPS agent. He was in an interview room, with two officers. Will and DeeDee asked where he was, and Detective Singleton and Detective Thompson approached them at the front desk.

Everyone was familiar with each other. They were led down the hall to interview room number nine. Ironic, nine was Trey's age. There, through the one-way mirror, sat their little boy with one hand cuffed to the table.

Trey had been changed into a white jumpsuit, not because of any other reason than his clothes were filthy. They needed his clothes to be processed. The Wilsons and Liz stood staring at Trey. The detective told them that they needed to hire a lawyer, he was going to be booked and sent to juvie, for the night. He would more than likely be arraigned in the morning and will be held in isolation.

Will asked if they could see him, and the detective said that they can. They followed him around to the side door.

When they entered, Trey jumped up and asked. "Mommy, daddy! Are you here to take me home.

DeeDee wanted to just scream, but she kept her cool. "No, honey, you can't go home right now."

He smiled, "I told you that I didn't like those boys." DeeDee ran from the room. Will asked his son, "What did you do?"

"I got rid of those boys." Will patted his son's hand and left the room too.

The detective told Will that he would be contacted with the time of his son's arraignment.

"Thank you, Detective." Will said and left to find his wife.

There was no mention of Rita Collins, that would be their lawyer's charge. Trey had been charged with two counts of murder. He was only nine, it's hard to say what the prosecution would request. This was a very delicate matter. It was also a very tragic matter. Was Trey mentally ill? Did he really kill his defenseless baby brothers? Are the two cases somehow tied together? Those are questions Detective Singleton and his crew were asking each other.

DeeDee thought she had no more tears, but she cried all the way home. Trey killed his brothers. She wailed; she beat the dashboard in the car.

"Will, he killed our innocent babies? He is out of his mind, he must be," DeeDee cried. "What has happened to him? He's gotten so big; I had not noticed how tall and thick he has become. Remember the doctor saying his pituitary gland has been affected?"

Will called his boss, Benny, as he would know a good lawyer and Benny was well connected in the community. Benny referred Will to Charles Miles, attorney-at-law. He was a juvenile criminal attorney, in practice for seventeen years. Will called him and left a message with his secretary.

"I will have him give you a call in the morning, Mr. Wilson," the secretary said.

"That will be fine," Will hang up.

Attorney Miles rang Will at eight-thirty a.m. He wanted the Wilsons to come to his office at noon. He had called juvie earlier; Trey was not going to be arraigned for a few days at the least. He asked them to bring a picture of Trey with them.

Will and DeeDee arrived promptly at noon, Atty. Miles was in the reception area, and he escorted them to his office.

"Please have a seat," the attorney said, and introductions were exchanged. Atty. Miles asked all the pertinent questions. He asked for the picture of Trey which was recent.

"This child is only nine," he said with a puzzled response.

"Yes," Will told him.

"He looks much older. I haven't been over to see him yet; however, I really need to know how your son obtained possession of a 45-caliber weapon?"

The Wilsons looked at each other. Will answered. "I have a 45; however, I have no idea why Trey would have it."

DeeDee chimed in. "Honey, are you sure you locked the gun box?"

"So much has gone on, no I am not sure, but I don't know where else he could have gotten one," said Will.

"The weapon was found in his backpack, when he was processed yesterday," the attorney revealed. "When will we be able to see our son?" Will asked.

"I am not sure but when we are done here, you can obtain that information from the juvenile detention center," the attorney said. "He's in serious trouble. The police department will be performing a ballistics test on the weapon, two bullets have been discharged, and there was gunshot residue on his hands, noting that Trey did fire it."

"It needs to be determined if the bullets match any crime scene," he continued. "I will get back to you on that issue. In the meantime, his defense will be not guilty by reason of insanity. From what you have told me, he has had serious mental issues. I will request his medical records. I will call you when I have more questions."

The attorney stood, buttoned his jacket, shook hands with the Wilsons, and escorted them out.

Will and DeeDee hadn't a chance to grieve for any of their children. Trevor and Travis had only been laid to rest a day earlier, and now this with Trey. He was in big trouble, they could only pray that the courts would consider the fact that he was merely a child, and they would be as lenient as possible. God only knew what the possibility of that could be.

They went to the Cory Juvenile Detention Center where Trey was housed to see their child. They waited patiently for him to be brought in. There was no contact. Trey sat behind a glass wall, handcuffed and shackled. He had an episode during the night and destroyed his cell. The guards were totally perplexed. Trey somehow managed to rip the bed from the wall. He was no longer allowed to be out of his cell without restraints.

Trey sat across from his parents; he didn't utter a word.

"Hello, honey, how are you?" DeeDee asked. Trey remained silent.

"Where did you get the gun?" Will asked his son.

"You gave it to me daddy," Trey answered.

"Absolutely, I did not," Will shot back at his son.

At that point, Trey had enough of the two of them, he leaped from his chair, lunged forward, banged the glass with his head and began to yell that them.

"Get me out of here! You hear me? Get me out of this place, I want to go home!"

The guards jumped into action; it took four of them to subdue the nine-year-old boy. Will and DeeDee left the visiting area in a hurry. They didn't even look back. Was he performing, or was he still a menace?

Back at the house, Carmen had made food for them. Shanna was still in a state of shock. Not eating much, not saying much. She was returning to school the next day. Liz had returned home and was now back at work but was on call if they needed her. Will and his wife sat quietly on the sofa. You could hear a pin drop; it was so quiet. They sat and cuddled with each other.

DeeDee began to cry. "I want my babies, I want all my babies, here with me."

"Trevor and Travis were dead, and Trey may as well have been. He would never be free again. At least we would be able to visit him, that was something," she said to her husband. "Thank God there was no death penalty in our state."

Attorneyy Miles called late in the evening. It was to let them know that Trey's arraignment would be in the morning, and they should be at the courthouse by 8:30 a.m. He would meet them outside of Courtroom B.

They tried to sleep but that was next to impossible. Will tossed and turned all night. DeeDee went to Trey's room to sit for a minute, and then to the nursery to do the same. She went back to bed to rejoin her husband.

"I still have you," she whispered in his ear. Will had dozed off; her words were uttered in vain.

When they returned home, they were discussing the visit with their eldest son, and their only living son.

"What do you think will happen to him," DeeDee asked Will.

"Well, if they find that he is mentally incompetent to stand trial, he may be sent to a mental institution for the rest of his life," answered Will. "If he's found guilty by reason of insanity, then he will still be sent to a mental institution. However, the Judge could find in his favor, to only serve a maximum sentence. Who knows how long that could be? I guess we will know sometime soon."

"Do you think Trey was putting on an act?" DeeDee asked Will.

"I don't know what I think at this point," answered Will. "To me, it seems premeditated. It appears that he gained our trust to get us to drop our guard, so that he could get close to the boys."

"How can you say that?" DeeDee would not allow herself to believe what she heard. "How could someone that she had carried for nine months, nurtured, and went through heck together is capable of planning and carrying out the murder of his two helpless brothers?"

"I believe that he committed cold-blooded murder, and he knew exactly what he was doing," said Will firmly.

"Yes, I believe that he is putting on a show, I begged you many times DeeDee to put him away, but you wouldn't listen. Now we must suffer the devastating truth," Will said.

"I rest my case. Only time will tell," DeeDee hung her head and prayed.

DeeDee felt some of the blame fell on her shoulders. I didn't listen to my husband; however, no one could have known this outcome. She rationalized with herself.

Liz came over in the evening, she wanted to get caught up with everything, and to know how her family was doing. Will and DeeDee had not heard of the murder of Rita Collins. They had been far too preoccupied and depressed to turn on the news.

"Are you all aware that that nurse that was stalking the house was murdered last week?" Liz asked.

"What?" Will was shocked.

"Well, it appears that she was found dead in her condo. She had blunt force trauma to her head, and she had been shot twice. They have no suspects currently."

Will thought about the gun in Trey's backpack and if they were related. He went upstairs to the lockbox in the bedroom. It was unlocked and his gun was gone.

I forgot to lock it back, that was months ago. No way of knowing how long it had been missing. I guess some of the blame should fall on me. My carelessness played a part in this tragedy. Will was thinking to himself. He went back to the living room to tell the others of his findings.

"I am so sorry honey; Trey took the gun. I didn't lock the box," he shared.

He felt awful. In addition to grieving for his boys, hating how he felt about his eldest son, and concern for his beautiful wife, he was overwhelmed with all sorts of grief.

The arraignment of Trey Allan Wilson was about to begin.

"All rise!" said the bailiff. "The Honorable Judge Carla Sheffield residing." The judge entered the court room and told them to be seated.

She called order to the court. "This is docket #1213 in the case of State of Mapleton Florida vs Trey Allen Wilson. How do you plead?"

Trey's attorney spoke. "On behalf of my client, we plead not guilty by reason of insanity."

Trey yelled from his chair. "No, I am guilty. I did whatever it is they say I did. I am guilty lady, you hear me, I am guilty."

The judge ordered Trey removed from the court room. "The plea is so noted. I will order that he be sent to the Mapleton Psychiatric Institute for an evaluation. He shall remain there until the seventh day of June; at such time I will make my ruling." All the evidence pointed to Trey. His fingerprints were on the pillow that smothered the twins, on the baseball bat that struck Carmen, on the door stop that struck Rita Collins, and the bullets were matched to that of the gun and slugs remove from Rita Collins' body. Trey was found guilty of three counts of first-degree murder. He would be sentenced on June 7, 2005.

Will and DeeDee were somewhat relieved that he was under lock and key for a substantial period. He, more than likely, will never see the light of day again without supervision. His trial would be a non-jury trial. He had already been proven guilty. His lawyer informed his parents he would come before the Judge on the said date, the doctors would present their findings, and, at such time he would be sentenced.

June 7 was four months away; his family would visit as often as possible. They had been informed that he was heavily sedated for his own protection, as well as the protection of those around him. His doses would be reduced depending on his progress. Trey had four psychiatrists; one was his main doctor. He prescribed his meds and had weekly sessions with him. The other three were staff psychiatrists, they monitored him daily.

Time appeared to be going by so slowly. DeeDee was getting better and stronger, as was Will, Liz, and Carmen. Shanna had gone to live with her grandmother. She no longer wanted to be in the house of horrors, as she referred to it. Carmen had made it home. She would stay to be of help to DeeDee. Will was working long hours; Liz resumed her life. DeeDee often thought of returning to teaching, but she didn't think she would be able to handle seeing all the happy kids right now. Maybe in the future, she thought to herself.

Will wasn't coming home on time anymore. Was he having an affair or was he avoiding what was behind his front door? They barely talked, seldom cuddled, only ate dinner together on weekends. They only went to visit Trey as a couple on Sundays. When they did go, Trey was so sedated, he could barely sit up straight. Will hated seeing his son that way. He never responded to his father, but he knew and loved seeing his mother. He was always happy to see Liz and Carmen on the rare times they visited. Will was very distant from his entire family. All that had gone wrong had taken its toll on everyone. DeeDee sat at home all day and watched TV. Carmen was in and out because she had started her home care nursing again.

DeeDee once broached the subject of trying to get pregnant again. Will was not having that. We had three and failed. We are not going to have another child. Absolutely not!Will was adamant. DeeDee never brought the subject up again.

June 7 arrived. They met Attorney Miles in the court room. He was at the defendant's table, but he took a minute when he saw them. The DA wanted what was best for the young boy. He would call for him to be detained in the asylum until he was twenty-five years old. At that time, if there were no other incidents then Trey could be reevaluated. Trey would not receive any prison time. Trey was escorted into the courtroom. He was in shackles and to his mom he looked alert. Not groggy like two days ago. Trey glanced back and when he saw his mom, he smiled. He sat quietly, until the bailiff asked them to stand. The judge entered, asked them to be seated, and read the docket just as before. The courtroom was as quiet as could be.

The State made its recommendations, the defense was fine with the DA's suggestions. Trey and his attorney stood, as well as the DA.

"Trey Allen Wilson, it is the order of this court that you remain in the custody of the Mapleton Psychiatric Institution for a period of forty years, or until such time that it is medically proven that you are no longer a threat to yourself or anyone else. Court is adjourned." She banged her gavel and stepped down from the bench.

DeeDee was in shock. Trey was taken away and his lawyer approached the family. "It was a harsh sentence, as you heard the DA only asked for twenty-five years. I wanted twenty but I never expected forty."

"Is there any possibility of him doing less time?" Will asked.

"We are going to appeal the verdict. But usually when it is not a jury trial, the sentence cannot be overturned or lessened. An appeal is automatic for me."

DeeDee didn't say anything. Will gave his wife a hug, and they left the courtroom with Liz and Carmen in tow.

"I will be in touch," Mr. Miles told them as they left.

Will had told his wife that he would not be going to visit every week anymore. DeeDee didn't respond. They all went their separate ways. It was a Friday morning, Will had taken the day off. He planned to go home and do nothing along with his wife. DeeDee thought she would make dinner and they could watch a movie. Will had other plans, he wanted to relax and be alone. DeeDee thought that odd, but she didn't rebut. They rarely kissed, hugged, or cuddled anymore. DeeDee was sure her husband was having an affair. She never asked and had only assumed.

Trey was sitting in the sunroom when his mother arrived. There were several orderlies stationed around. It was a very nice facility, thank God Will had great insurance. Trey gave his mother a big hug, he was not restrained. His medication was working. He had not had an episode in a week. Two weeks ago, he tackled a patient he decided he didn't like. Trey explained that he was messing around; thankfully no one was hurt. The two made up and all was well. Trey often told himself that he was going to be a good boy so one day he would be free. He has unfinished business. His doctors would never know the real Trey Allan Wilson, nor would his parents.

DeeDee returned to her empty home, Carmen was still at work. She decided to go visit the twin's graves, she always went after her visit with Trey. She watched a movie after and had a late lunch at a little bistro. DeeDee was alone most of the time, but she had gotten to the place where she didn't mind at all.

Will came home one day and told DeeDee that he wanted a divorce.

"What, a divorce? I didn't know you were so unhappy," she said to her husband.

"I have met someone else, and I love her. She is pregnant," Will revealed.

She was sure that she was dreaming.

"Honey, I still love you, but things haven't been the same since the babies. I never thought that I wanted more children."

"Will, you're pushing fifty years old. I asked you years ago and you said no more children."

"This wasn't planned, it just happened."

"You are standing there, telling me this as if you were talking about the weather. Is this midlife crisis?" DeeDee couldn't even be upset. "I have lost my children. You are leaving me. So now where do I go from here?"

"I will make sure that you don't want for anything," Will told his soon-to-be ex-wife.

"I have felt for some time that you were slipping away. Your lack of affection, your late nights, and it seems that you have given up on your son. I haven't given up on Trey."

"I cannot forgive or forget what he has done."

"You must forgive, not for Trey, but so that you can move on. But I see you are not having a problem moving on. How old is she?" DeeDee asked.

"She is thirty-three, if that should matter," responded Will.

"It doesn't matter, Will. I was just curious."

DeeDee seemed to always be in a state of shock. God, you have kept me through losing my children, you will keep me through this as well. Thank you, Father, for loving me. Please forgive him and continue to protect him always, Amen. Will went about his way and DeeDee retired to her room to watch mindless TV.

DeeDee went to visit Trey, he was getting better and also getting older, Trey was now seventeen years old, he had been locked away for eight years. DeeDee hadn't missed a visit. She visits twice during the week and on Sundays. She told Trey on one of their visits that she and his father were divorced. They had been divorced for two years before she told Trey.

Trey made it known to his mother that he hated his dad for leaving her alone. Trey never mentioned him again, nor did DeeDee. In his mind, he could see himself stabbing his father to death, if he ever got out, he would. Trey was still very much mentally ill. He was playing the game, so he thought. He was good at it too. DeeDee left Trey in good spirits, and she was in good spirits also. Will had remarried and had a two-year-old daughter. They stayed in touch. She loved his little girl. The two got along well.

DeeDee had gone back to teaching full-time. A substitute took over her class on the days she would go to visit Trey. Will came around to see her often, they laughed and talked about the good old days. The days before all the drama and sadness.

"We were happy back then," Will reminisced. DeeDee agreed. They had wine and enjoyed the company of each other. She remembered how she missed him so, when he first left. But God had gotten her over another mountain. Life goes on.

When Will began to come over more often, DeeDee became suspicious. She didn't say anything. She was very observant so if something was amiss, it would reveal itself soon.

He came in one day, sat at the kitchen table of the house DeeDee remolded when he left. Too many memories, she thought. The two of them were having coffee, Will looked at his ex-wife and noticed how beautiful she still was, even at fifty-five. Will spoke first.

"DeeDee, I want to come back home."

DeeDee tried not to, but she laughed so hard tears were coming down her face. Will sat there stone-faced.

"I don't see what's so funny, DeeDee," Will said.

"Will you have got to be kidding me. There is nothing for you to come back to, the woman you left is long gone. The home you left is new. I don't see you in that light anymore.

"It doesn't work like that. God got me, us, some tough times. There is no way I will ever go back.

"But I love you, I have never stopped loving you," Will answered.

"I love you too, Will. It's not a romantic love." said DeeDee. "We will always be friends but there is nothing else, it is over for me."

Will hung his head, in shame. She was so over him. She wished him no ill will. All the best, she told him. Will left feeling broken. Better him than DeeDee.

Trey was turning twenty-one in a few weeks. DeeDee had gotten permission to give him a get-together in the sunroom. She had ordered a cake and of ice cream. His favorite since he was a boy was red velvet cake with vanilla ice cream. Yummy, yummy. That's what he would always say when he liked a certain foods.

She placed the cake in the middle of the table, the ice cream was in a cooler. Everyone gathered around and sang Happy Birthday. DeeDee had two candles, two and one. Trey blew them out and made a wish under his breath. Trey stood six feet and four inches tall and he weighed 220 pounds. He was super handsome, looking like a mix of his mother and father.

Will hadn't seen his son in twelve years. It was a very nice birthday. Trey was happy, DeeDee gave him a hug, and told him that she would see him in two days. I love you, they both said it at the same time. His mother was gone again.

Trey was planning his great escape. He had to get out, he had work to do. He would go and be back before anyone discovered he was missing. Trey had stolen a bus pass from one of the orderly's jackets. He also had stashed a uniform that he had stolen from the supply room. He was a big guy and most of the orderly's had a large size as well. He was allowed to wear his own shoes if they didn't have strings. The ones his mother bought him were slip-ons which might create a problem if he got into a situation where he had to run. It was a week away, he wanted to continue planning. He couldn't make any mistakes. He also had to make sure it was a non-visiting day. His mother came faithfully.

Okay, that's enough brain exercise for one day. Overload is not good. It made him very anxious, he thought. When he got like that, they gave him a higher dosage of medication, which made him foggy. Trey liked having a clear head, he did not like being medicated. He would hide his pills in his upper lip until he was out of sight. Then he would spit them out and put them in his pocket. Hiding meds is the oldest trick in the book, he doesn't know why no one checked him thoroughly. Trey was very smart. He had gotten away with murdering three people. He knew he would not be sent to the big house; he was fine in the psychiatric facility. More freedom after they get you under control. Trey had to keep playing his game. He would often think, *I don't know why I am so evil, I had wonderful parents, especially my mother. I love her so much, and she loves me. My father, not so much.*

DeeDee was having an exceptional day, her class was this group of well-behaved girls and boys. She returned to the classroom four years ago, after divorce was final. Teaching was her passion. DeeDee gave it up to stay at home with Trey. She always dreamt of being back in the classroom. *Yes, today was a good day. Thank you, my heavenly father, I give you all the honor, praise, and glory. Amen.*

Will was miserable, he was so unhappy with his life. He still saw his daughter, but he was fifty-five and soon to be twice divorced. He left his wife for greener pastures, those pastures turned out not to be so green after all. She had moved on, but he still wanted her back. He would be patient. He had been promoted to general manager. The job was going very well. He made lots of money, had a lovely condo on the water, drove a nice car, but Will was not happy.

There is an old saying, "You made your bed, now you must lay in it." He wished he could turn things around with his ex-wife. He realized how strong and God-fearing she was and had always been. He began to pray for God to listen to him; however, He won't answer until he is ready. He realized that you can't pray when you want something. Prayer is a ritual. Will found time to pray only when he needed or wanted something. That's not how it works, buddy. He knew his DeeDee was a praying woman.

Liz had tried contacting her sis and former brother-in-law on several occasions. She had not talked to her sister in over a month. She would go by the house later. She knew DeeDee was back in the classroom. She was happy for her, but she missed her. She had been upset with Will because of the way that he disrespected his sister. She was glad that DeeDee had gotten on with her life. Liz knocked on the door and rang the doorbell at the same time. DeeDee looked through the peephole and opened the door when she saw it was Liz.

"Oh, my goodness! It's so good to see you," Liz told her sister.

"I have missed you too, sis. Let's have a play date. We can get together and have a sleep over to catch up on old times."

"That sounds like a plan. You just let me know when and where," DeeDee told Liz.

DeeDee had gone for her visit and wouldn't be back for three days. She told Trey that she had an appointment that she could not miss. Trey was fine with that because he could put his plan in motion.

He decided to leave after the shift changed. That way, he would be present when night check came around. Trey left the facility through a hole in the wall that led to the outside. He was out, he was careful not to bring attention to himself. Trey walked down three blocks to the farther bus stop, hopped on the bus and was off. He got off and walked around. He ventured out into a ritzy neighborhood, with lots of condos and town homes. He knew where it was.

Trey had researched his father's whereabouts on the internet in the computer room at the hospital. He went directly there. He accomplished his mission, walked the six blocks to the bus stop, got off three stops from the hospital and eased back in. No one ever knew he had left.

Will did not show up for work, nor did he answer his phone. That was out of character for him. Benny, his boss called 911 to do a welfare check. The police went to Will's condo, knocked several times, but there was no answer. He looked through the window, nothing seemed out of place. He went to the leasing office and asked to be let into Mr. Wilson's unit. The manager gave him the master key and took the officer back to the condo. They entered, the officer checked the entire place out, no sign of Will, but his car was still in his parking space. That seemed odd, maybe he went for a run, the manager closed the door and they left.

Trey had made his escape without a hitch. He was proud of himself. He was on cloud nine. *I will be glad to see mother,* Trey was thinking out loud. He had to watch that because he didn't want to say something out loud that shouldn't be heard. He tossed the uniform down the incinerator, wiped the prints from the ID, threw it on the floor as if someone had dropped it, went back to his room, and climbed into bed. Trey laid in bed with his hands behind his head, staring at the ceiling, with a sinister grin on his face. I must do that again, that was exhilarating. He turned over and went to sleep.

Days went by and it was time for his mother's visit. Trey always looked forward to time with his mom. He recently stopped calling her mommy. Mom was more appropriate at his age. DeeDee walked into the sunroom and there sat Trey, he was unusually happy.

"Hello mother, mother," Trey only called her mother on special occasions.

"Hi, honey," DeeDee greeted her son. "How are you doing?"

"I am wonderful," he told his mother. "How are you?"

"I'm well."

They chatted for an hour. When it was time for DeeDee to leave, Trey became agitated.

"I am not ready for you to leave, mommy," Trey spoke in a childlike voice.

"Visiting hours are over, but I will see you in two days."

"Okay, mom," Her was back to Trey. DeeDee left and blew him a kiss on the way out.

When DeeDee thought back about the visit, Trey seemed to be all over the place. One minute he is calling her mother, the next he is calling her mom and then mommy, he hasn't called her mommy in at least a year. His voice changed. I so hope that he is alright. If not, he is in the right place, DeeDee thought.

Days had gone by, and Will had not been heard from. The police went back to his condo, this time a neighbor reported a foul smell coming from his unit. There were two police officers. The manager took them, they entered, but before they walked in, the stench was unbearable. One of the officers stepped back, saying it was the smell of death. The odor was coming from the coat closet, which had only been scanned on the prior welfare check, and it wasn't searched. When the closet was opened, they knew the smell of decaying flesh. Behind several coats was a bloody sheet. They called it in, the detectives arrived, along with forensics. The sheet was uncovered; and there lay Will Wilson's dead body.

The medical examiner arrived and found that Will had stab wounds everywhere, there was so much blood. They bagged Will's body and put him in the truck. The medical examiner told the detective that he would let him know the cause of death as soon as possible. Forensics finished dusting for prints. The crime scene was wrapped up and police tape placed out front and on the door of his unit.

DeeDee was notified. She was listed as the next of kin. The detective asked if she would come to the police station.

"You were listed as the next of kin to William Wilson."

"Why is Will at the police station?" she asked.

"He is deceased," the detective told her.

"Deceased? What are you talking about?" DeeDee could not believe what she was hearing.

"We need you to identify the body. If you come to the station, one of our officers will take you over to the medical examiner's office."

This was a repeat of a time that DeeDee didn't want to remember.

"I don't know what to say."

"Please come to the station as soon as possible."

"I am on my way."

It was six-thirty in the evening, DeeDee got there as quickly as possible. She was taken to the morgue, the medical examiner rolled the body up to the window. DeeDee felt faint, she caught herself on the railing. The sheet was pulled down to the neck, he had a cut to his ear. She stared at the body, the officer asked who he was. DeeDee confirmed that it'sy her ex-husband, William Wilson.

"Thank you, Ms. Wilson. Sorry for your loss." He took her back to her car and she returned home.

DeeDee rang Liz, it was about eight p.m. by the time she returned home.

"Hey sis, what's up? You alright?" Liz asked her sister.

"No, I am not alright. I just returned from the morgue, I had to identify Will's body. He is dead, Liz, dead."

"Oh, my goodness! What happened?"

"He was murdered. They found him in his closet, he had been out of work for a week. The police did a welfare check, and they found his body."

"Oh my, oh my, do you want me to come over?"

"No, sis. You have work tomorrow and so do I, Anyway, Carmen is here. Let's talk tomorrow, I will update you then."

Trey was relishing the events that took place at his father's house. He found an unlocked window, climbed in. His father had fallen asleep on the sofa. There was a statue of a ceramic elephant beside the end table, Trey picked it up and brought it down on his father's head. He made sure that he hit him on the forehead so that any blood would roll down his face opposed to running down by his near ear. Trey didn't want any blood on the sofa.

He removed all the coats from the hallway walk-in closet. Then, he went to find plastic bags. He placed plastic bags by the closet door, after which Trey dragged his father over and into the back of the closet. He placed the bags over his father's body, from his neck down, and with the butcher's knife he retrieved from the kitchen, he began to stab and stab. He made sure not to get any blood on his clothes. He had covered himself with plastic bags as well. When he was sure his father was dead, he then placed the sheet over his body and placed the contents of the closet back inside. Trey removed all the plastic, stuffed them in another bag, closed the closet door and left. Everything went into the incinerator back at the hospital.

DeeDee contacted Will's wife. There divorce was not final yet, but she needed to take care of Will from then on out. DeeDee removed herself from the situation. She informed his wife as to where he was and gave her the detective's contact information. Any further questions should be directed to either the medical examiner or the police. She told her that she was sorry for her loss.

Back at the Mapleton Psychiatric Hospital, Trey was waiting for his mom to come visit. DeeDee didn't know how she would tell her son of his fathers' death. A light went off in DeeDee's head, *Could Trey have had anything to do with this? She shook the thought off, impossible, he was under lock and key. Under constant supervision. Not possible!* She sat behind the wheel for a second to gather her thoughts. DeeDee let out a sigh, *How will I tell my son that his father has been murdered?*

The phone rang as she was getting out of her car. It was Liz.

"Hello honey, how are you doing?"

"I just heard on the news about Will. Where are you," she asked.

"I am at the hospital. It is my visiting day with Trey. I don't know how I am going to give him the news."

"Do you want me to come to this visit with you? I can be there in fifteen minutes," Liz offered.

"Okay, I will wait in the lobby. See you shortly," Liz hung up.

Liz arrived and the two went together to see Trey. Trey was waiting patiently for his mother, and when he saw his Auntie, his expression changed. He did not expect to see her. He wanted to tell his mother what he had done. After all, he had done it for his mother. Auntie Liz had ruined everything. They sat down with Trey; they both gave him a hug. DeeDee spoke first.

"Trey, honey, I have some very bad news to tell you." Trey glanced at his Auntie Liz, rolled his eyes, looked back at his mom and asked her. "What's wrong?"

"It's your father, baby, he has been killed." Trey sat there expressionless.

"Oh, that's too bad, but he probably deserved whatever happened to him. Was he in a car crash," Trey asked nonchalantly.

"No, he was stabbed to death in his home."

"Did someone break in?"

"The police don't have the details yet. You don't seem upset."

"I am not upset, I hated him for how he treated you. But to be honest, I have always hated him. I don't want to talk about him anymore. You both can leave now; I don't want you to visit anymore."

The orderly came over to escort Trey back to his room. The two sisters sat in shock. "Let's go," DeeDee took her sister by the arm, and they left the sunroom.

DeeDee and Liz went to the cafeteria to get some coffee and chat before going their separate ways.

"I do not know what to make of what just happened," DeeDee was dumbfounded.

"He didn't break a sweat," Liz said. "He was as calm as a cucumber."

"I hope he will be alright," was DeeDee's motherly response.

"I would say he will be just fine," Liz responded. "What was that he asked? Then he had the nerve to dismiss us like we were bad kids or something. I am done," Liz said. "I will never come here again. He even had the nerve to roll is eyes at me, sis. He is still not well; I am no doctor, but something is still very wrong, and, in my opinion, he is right where he needs to be."

"Please don't be like that, sis," DeeDee was feeling bad about the entire incident. They finished their coffee and left.

Detective Singleton was in his office looking over the medical examiner's report. Will had been stabbed forty-two times, he had stab wounds everywhere but the top of his head and the soles of his feet. His face was untouched as well. The wounds were so deep that they went from his chest to his spine. *It is my job to find the killer,* he thought to himself. *I have no suspects and no clues. Who was so angry to do this to another human being? I have nothing to go on, no places to start. Hopefully, the perp left fingerprints somewhere. Will had been dead for almost a week when his body was found.*

Will's body had been released to the funeral home, the same one they hired for Trevor and Travis's bodies. The service would be held on a Wednesday, the following week. Will's wife, soon-to-be ex-wife, had taken care of the arrangements. She didn't ask DeeDee to help and DeeDee was fine with that. DeeDee wasn't keen on the idea of attending the services, but she would go pay her respects to her ex-husband, the father of her children. Liz and Carmen would attend with her.

The service lasted an hour and fifteen minutes. DeeDee timed it on her cell phone. Will had made lots of friends, and he had quite a few associates. His boss Benny said a few words, along with some other people DeeDee didn't know. DeeDee, Liz, and Carmen opted out of going to the cemetery. Instead, they went back to DeeDee's house and had their own small repass. They ate, drank, and caught up on old times. It was good for them to gather after such a somber day. The girls decided they would have a girl's night once a month, the place and time to be announced. They all said their goodbyes, after hours of catching up and enjoying each other's company. Carmen and DeeDee still shared her house. It was a perfect fit still. No problems. Shanna, Carmen's daughter, stayed over from time to time. Neither woman was dating, but they okay with that.

Trey was still irritated that his mother brought his Auntie Liz along on the last visit. His mom shouldn't have done that, now he would never let her in on his secret. Trey had been placed in solitary confinement because he attacked one of the female patients on another ward. He had also been medicated heavily again. He told the nurse that he did not want a visit from his mother. *Tell her I don't want any visitors when she comes.* Trey always seemed to be angry. Nothing seemed to please him. There was no one to tell that he had killed his father, Trey felt he was about to explode in the literal sense. Everyone knew that a person wouldn't explode because they didn't tell a secret. Trey was thinking to himself.

DeeDee arrived for her visit, but she was turned away. Her son did not want to see her, this was the first time in all his time away. She was disappointed; however, not overly so. She wasn't sure she wanted to see him anyway. DeeDee hadn't been feeling herself since Will's funeral. She had been feeling lost somehow. She prayed even more often, which helped tremendously. Today was one of those days. She didn't stress over the fact that she couldn't see Trey. She went home to just chill.

It was 5:30 a.m. when DeeDee's phone rang. It was Trey's doctor at the Mapleton Psychiatric Hospital. She answered the phone groggy and confused.

"Hello, hello, may I speak with Ms. Wilson?"

"This is she," said DeeDee.

"Ms. Wilson, this is Dr. Sander, Trey's doctor, calling from the hospital concerning your son."

"Yes, Doctor... Is everything okay?" DeeDee asked.

"No, I am afraid not. Trey has somehow managed to escape."

DeeDee gasped into the phone, she was at a loss for words.

"If you should hear from him, would you please contact me immediately?"

"Absolutely, I will," she said before they ended the conversation. DeeDee, no sooner than that call ended, got another call. This time, it was from Detective Thompson. He began to say that Trey had committed several crimes at the hospital, and they had reason to believe that he murdered his father.

"That's not possible"! DeeDee screamed in his ear. "My son was under lock and key. No Detective! Please tell me it's not true."

"I am afraid it is true. We are still investigating his father's murder. We will let you know when we have finished our investigation. In the meantime,

I would say keep your doors locked and if he should come to your home, call 911. He is believed to be armed and considered dangerous."

Trey had escaped through the same hole in the wall that he had created on his first escape. Only this time, he didn't cover his tracks. He left the hole uncovered. He must have been in a big hurry. Before leaving, he managed to kill two and wound another. He had been ranting all day about his work not being finished. He was mumbling something about his mother and those boys. Trey was on his way to murder his mother.

Trey was still clad in jeans and a blue sweatshirt, one that his mother had given him during his stay. He was wearing his slip-ons and a grey jacket that he had stolen from someone's locker on the basement level. Trey wasn't supposed to be in the basement. No one knew but Trey had been given far too much freedom. He had been pretending for years. He had been able to fool the doctors, the nurses, and anyone involved in his treatment. There were hundreds of doses of his medication hidden under his mattress.

DeeDee called Carmen from the basement and then she called Liz, who told her that she was on her way over. DeeDee and Carmen sat on the sofa watching the news. Trey was once again plastered over the TV screen. He wasn't a child anymore; he was an adult. He was still her son no matter what he had done. DeeDee told this to Carmen, Carmen advised her not to talk like that around her sister.

"I really don't understand the statement either, DeeDee," Carmen said. "Trey is a murderer. He killed his own father, for heavens sake. I hope that you are not condoning his behavior."

DeeDee and Carmen had become as close as sisters. "You've been instructed not to open the door if he should knock. He may be after you."

The doorbell rang and a knock came at the same time. DeeDee knew it was her sister, but she wasn't taking any chances. She asked who it was and then looked through the peephole. It was Liz. She quickly opened the door and just a quickly closed the door behind Liz. Carmen went to the kitchen to make coffee. It was now seven-thirty a.m. The three women sat in the living room glued to the TV screen. Trey was a wanted man.

The phone rang again, it was Detective Singleton this time. He told DeeDee he was sending over a patrol car, because it was believed her life was in danger.

"That's fine, Detective, thank you," DeeDee answered. But to Liz, she said, "They must be delusional if they think for a minute that my son would harm me."

"If they think that he may have murdered his dad, he might want to kill you as well," Liz said but DeeDee wasn't hearing her sister.

Trey was outside of his mother's door; he tried to peek in, but the blinds were shut. He walked around to different windows, but they were all locked. *I will just lay and wait; she must come out eventually.* He found a place in the flowerbed and made himself as comfortable as he could considering the circumstances. Trey was hungry and thirsty, it was mid-September, even though it wasn't cold during the day in Florida, the nights got cold. Trey was starting to feel the cold.

The search was on for the serial killer. Trey Allan Wilson, now twenty-three years old. The families of the murdered victims were in the lobby of the hospital. They were being shielded from the reporters. Trey had bludgeoned to death a female nurse and a doctor. He tried to kill and orderly, but he didn't die since the orderly's injuries were not life-threatening. Trey had in his possession several knives that he had taken from the kitchen. He had access to quite a few of the rooms around the building. He was very cunning and very dangerous. He needed to be caught as soon as possible.

Trey had fallen asleep. He awoke when he saw flashing blue lights, got up from the flowerbed, and eased his way over to the yard next door. He didn't see any lights on in the house, so he tried a window and it opened. He slowly raised the window that was without a screen, and climbed in. The Clements used to live in the house. He had been gone so long he wasn't sure if they still lived there or not. It was dark so he needed to be careful. Trey heard the knock on the door, it was the police. They were going door to door, warning everyone that was home.

No one answered the door to the Clements home. He felt his way around. Hoping he was alone. He was starting to warm up. He wanted to eat and have something to drink. He felt his way to the kitchen, he felt the stove, then the refrigerator. Ah food, he thought. He opened the fridge and chugged down a carton of orange juice. He returned the carton to the shelf. He saw a packet of turkey sandwich meat. He scarfed that down. Trey felt a little better. He grabbed another package of meat and two bottles of water stuffed them in his pockets. He was okay for a few minutes.

DeeDee, Liz, and Carmen were still glued to the TV. They all had called off work. The cop cars were stationed outside. The ladies felt safe, but DeeDee was not in fear of her son. "He would never hurt me," she told the girls. "My child loves me."

"Okay," Liz said. "Okay sis. I hope you are right."

Trey entered the basement, but he wasn't alone. There was a dog, a German Shepherd, and it chased Trey up the steps. He reached the top and shut the door. Lights came on upstairs, Trey hurried back to the window, which he had left open, and climbed back out into the yard. He accidentally nicked his leg with one of the knives. Just a nick, he shrugged it off. He still saw the blinking lights and laid low for a while. He wanted to go knock on his mother's door, but that was too risky. He wanted to go home.

The detectives were winding things up at the crime scene. It was still chaotic but coming to a quite calm. The task at hand was to find Trey before he hurt someone else. He would head over to the Wilson home to get as much information as they could. It was noon, and it was warming up again. They arrived at Ms. Wilson's door with a hardy knock. Liz went to the door, asked who it was, and peeped through the peephole before opening. One can never be too careful.

Trey was lurking in the backyard of his mother's home. He heard voices but not clearly. He made out his mother's voice and he began to cry. He wanted to yell at her and have her hold him like she used to. But he knew that was not possible anymore. His time was coming to an end. Trey backed himself into a corner and he didn't know how to get out. He had essentially dug his own grave. His life was never going to be the same again. He had a chance before he started killing again. He was doomed, his mommy may have well been on the moon, because it was out of her hands. *I want her dead too. I told her I didn't want those boys; she didn't listen. Mommy had to die, too. It's her fault, everything is all her fault.*

Detectives Singleton and Thompson were allowed in after being cleared by Liz. They went to the kitchen, the ladies took chairs, and the detectives stood. Carmen served coffee for everyone. Singleton and Thompson took out their pads and started writing. They concluded the interview and were about to leave when there was a noise at the back door. Guns drawn, the two stealthily proceeded to check out the noise. The flowerbed had bed disturbed. There were footprints in the flowerbed. Large footprints,

DeeDee began to sob. "He's been here," she yelled. "My son has been here, oh my God! Trey were, are you?"

Liz held her sister and they both cried, Carmen cried too.

Singleton radioed to the patrolmen that the suspect is in the area and for units to be on the lookout. "Be vigilant. He is very dangerous."

DeeDee heard that and fell to the ground. "Please don't hurt him, please don't hurt my boy." She begged them not to hurt Trey.

Trey had eluded the police once again; he was nowhere to be found. Several patrol units were diligently searching for the lone killer.

DeeDee was inconsolable. She wanted her son, she believed that he had changed. "The medication was working. He was a good boy."

"He is no longer a boy," Liz said to her sister. "And he has done some terrible things. It's time that he pays."

The death penalty had been reinstated. If trey was found guilty of the charges against him, he could be put to death. It wasn't clear if the insanity plea would work a second time around.

Trey was still on the run; the police department was overwhelmed with calls of sightings. Nothing panned out. "We will find him," Singleton told his partner. "It's only a matter of time."

Trey had doubled back to his mother's house, but there were cops everywhere He didn't stand a chance in hell of getting close to her. But he was content peeking through the bushes. Trey wanted nothing more than to put his hands around her neck until she was dead. After all he was insane!

DeeDee wanted to return to work, but she wouldn't be able to without security. She was a prisoner in her own home. The blinds remained closed all the time. Liz and Carmen had returned to work. Trey was a large figure, hard to miss, but he was able to maintain his cover, as it were. Carmen was a home nurse for an elderly gentleman. She worked from eight a.m. until four p.m., when her shift ends, and another nurse takes over. There were three shifts. Carmen was leaving after her shift and, out of nowhere, she was being dragged to the woods next door to the house where she worked. She was overpowered, a hand over her mouth, and he took her into the woods. Carmen struggled but she didn't stand a chance against 220 pounds of Trey Allan Wilson. He broke her neck and left her in the woods, like trash. He killed her because he couldn't get to his mother. Carmen had no idea she was being stalked.

DeeDee got the news, and she was absolutely devastated.

"Words cannot explain how I feel," she told Liz on the phone." I want you to come over here and stay until they catch him. I believe he will hurt or even worse kill us both if he gets the chance. He killed sweet Carmen. I am overwhelmed, Liz, I don't know how much more I can take. My heart is hurting. God, please continue to pour your strength into me. Help me, Father, please." She prayed.

My son is a killer, a serial killer, he has no limits. Wherever you are, you need to be caught, taken off the streets. I am so sorry I failed you, my child. Please forgive me. DeeDee wrote this in her journal. DeeDee was at a loss for words, this wasn't the first time, it undoubtedly would not be the last.

Trey went about his business. He found a homeless camp where an older man took him in. Trey followed him to the dumpsters and trash cans to find food. They also went to restaurants, because they threw out good stuff the man told him. Trey thought they would never find me out here. I am home, free, he said to himself. Trey seemed to be okay with his new friend. He had no complaints. How does one go from a loving family, great home, mother and father adored him, to becoming a serial killer, and living on the street?

Trey Allan Wilson's time is running out. The police were searching in homeless camps also, only Trey wasn't aware that they were. The police were out in full force. Looking for the twenty-three-year-old serial killer.

DeeDee didn't know what to do. She still loved her son and always would, but she was terrified of what would happen to him when he was captured. *Would they shoot him on sight? Would they apprehend him safely? She was also afraid of him; he was killing off anyone close to her. Was she or Liz next?* These thoughts looped around DeeDee's head. The cops were not letting her out of their sight.

Trey hadn't given up on trying to get to his mother. *She must die too!* This was always on his mind.

Trey made the mistake of venturing out of the homeless campground. He wanted real food; so, he went to panhandle. Trey decided to beg for money. Big mistake, Trey Allan Wilson, big mistake. He found the perfect spot, or so he thought, in front of a coffee shop, one that the police frequented. He stood with his cup in hand, and he was noticed immediately. The police officer saw him and called for backup. He wasn't going to try to apprehend Trey alone.

Sirens blazing, blue lights flashing, Trey was thinking, what's going on. He had no idea the performance was his last one. Cops jumped from cars, ran up on him, tackled and subdued him. He made it seem like they had the wrong person, his face was on every police car, even in the inside of police hats. It was over for Trey Allan Wilson. His time had run out!

Trey was brought to his feet, read his rights, handcuffed, and placed in the back of the police cruiser, for the second and last time of his short life.

Before he was taken to be processed, he was placed in shackles. Shackles had been a part of his other life, prior to the psychiatric hospital. It was all very familiar to him. There was a frenzy of reporters at the police station. Mics being shoved in his face, Trey remained quiet. DeeDee was helping to prepare for Carmen's service. She was on the phone, and when she looked up and there was her child being escorted into the police station.

Carmen had been cremated. There was going to be a small memorial service in honor of her life. She was a good girl. DeeDee was going to miss her so much. My son had ruined everything. He was picking her loved ones off one by one. I wish I knew where we went wrong. Was he just plain evil? Was he really with a sick mind and out of control?

It seemed to DeeDee that he was on some sort of mission to destroy anything in his path. Or was he only out to make her life a living hell. Either way, he had succeeded in killing her without even committing the act.

She rang Liz and gave her and update on what's been going on. She asked her to come and go to the station with her. She left the planning for Carmen to her mother and daughter. She had to go see about her son. Liz arrived and they rode together while Liz drove. DeeDee was a nervous wreck. What would she say if they let her see him? He was disheveled on the news. His clothes were dirty, and he had a slight bit of hair on his face. He looked homeless. Little did DeeDee know he was.

Trey had been processed and was in one of the interview rooms waiting to be interviewed. DeeDee was not allowed to see him until he was charged and booked. That would be sometime in the next day or so. Liz drove her home and stayed with her.

"I need to get him a lawyer," she told her sister.

"A lawyer?" Liz shouted at her. "What is wrong with you? Let him get a public defender. He doesn't deserve your hard-earned money put out for his defense. He is a serial killer, DeeDee, he probably would have killed us too if he could have gotten to us. He's off the street. God willing, he will never see the light of day again." Liz had said her peace. She was done.

Detective Singleton and his partner interrogated Trey for hours. After Trey was done being pushed around, as he called it, refusing to answer any questions, he demanded his lawyer. Singleton asked him if he had a lawyer, he answered no.

"My mother will hire one for me. I have one phone call; I want it now. I know my rights." When he lawyered up, the interview was terminated. He was transferred to lock up. He was behind bars, where he would most likely spend the rest of his life, if he didn't get the death penalty.

Trey made his one phone call to his mother. DeeDee was resting So Liz answered the phone.

"Where is my mother? I need to speak to her," Liz took the phone out of ear shot; she didn't want to disturb her sister.

She told Trey through the gritting of her teeth. "You listen to me, Trey, you have done enough damage to this family, you will not speak to your mother, and don't you ever call here again. I hope they lock you up and throw away the key."

She slammed down the phone and went back to the living room where DeeDee was resting on the sofa.

"Who was that?" DeeDee asked. "No one, sweetie, wrong number."

Trey was livid, he was seething, he went into a state of absolute rage. Banging the phone on the wall while still handcuffed and shackled. But that didn't stop the lunatic from destroying anything that he could get his hands on. It took seven guards to restrain him. He was spitting, trying to kick. They had to place the spit hood over his head. He was strapped in the safety resistant chair. Trey was out of control once again. He was exactly where he needed to be.

Trey was transferred to the mental facility. In the jail, he would remain there under continuous supervision. His arraignment must be virtual since he wasn't allowed out of his cell. He was assigned to a public defender. His defense was uncertain as to a plea. Attorney Steinberg was assigned to Trey's case. He read the files on his client and all he could do was shake his head. *Was he reading this correctly, this twenty-four-year-old man who was barely out of diapers was a serial killer? Convicted of three counts, and four more pending, if proven guilty of the latest murders, he could be put to death.*

Attorney Steinberg removed his glasses and rubbed his forehead. He let out a sigh, this will be a difficult case. He had once been found guilty and sentenced to forty years in the asylum, he had his work cut out for him.

Liz had talked DeeDee out of hiring an attorney. It was a waste of money for sure. She wanted to see her child.

"After all that he has done, he is still my child and I love him. I hate what he has become but he will always be my son," she cried. DeeDee was not in the best of health, the stress of all that had gone wrong had taken its toll on her. She wasn't getting any younger either. Liz had rented out her house and moved in with her sister to keep an eye on her and to help her if she needed help.

DeeDee retired after Trey escaped. Most of her days were spent in the house, she read a lot and listened to music. The music was good medicine for her. Liz was working part-time. She was the cook and the maid; she teased her sister. She didn't mind at all, the two of them were all the immediate family left. Though they had many friends and distant family, DeeDee wasn't up for company most of the time.

Trey met with his attorney to discuss his options, which were slim to none. The first meeting was tense for both. Trey was brought down to the visitation room while still in the restraint chair, they were some distance from each other. The attorney made it very clear that there would be no spitting. He had read and found out everything there was to know about his client. He asked Trey how he wanted to plead. Trey told him not guilty by reason of insanity. The attorney looked at Trey with a puzzled expression.

"Do you think you are insane?" Steinberg asked.

"It's not what I think, it's what you must prove, you are my attorney, so prove that I am not in my right mind." He asked to be taken back to his cell. Steinberg didn't move, he watched as Trey was rolled back to his cell. Steinberg needed to talk to Trey's mother.

The DA was going for the maximum sentence, the Death Penalty. That was Trey Allan Wilson's only option in his mind. He was a menace to society and there could not be the slightest chance that he might be back on the streets ever again. In his opinion, Trey would never stop killing.

Attorney Steinberg met with DeeDee and Liz at his office in town. DeeDee wasn't at all happy about not being able to see her son since he had been incarcerated all most two months. Steinberg explained that her son was in solitary confinement because of his unruly behavior. He shared to her that Trey had been very abusive to him and to the staff at the jail. DeeDee understood but she still didn't like it.

"How is he?" she asked Steinberg.

"Oh, he is just fine, as belligerent as can be. I will ask for him to be re-evaluated by the psychiatrist again. But the truth be known, Ms. Wilson, I don't think that is going to fly this time. The DA is asking for the death penalty."

"The death penalty, I thought the death penalty was no longer enforced in this state," DeeDee was shaking.

"The Death Penalty was reinstated two years ago, Ms. Wilson. If Trey pleads not guilty by reason of insanity, the courts will request that he undergo several evaluations."

"Yes, I am aware of the evaluations, he underwent them before."

"Well, if he is found competent to stand trial, his chances are very slim of being found not guilty."

"When he will be arraigned," DeeDee asked.

"He's going to be arraigned tomorrow morning. However, he will not be brought to the courtroom. The arraignment will be on teleprompter. You are allowed in the courtroom; however, you can't see him. You won't be able to talk to him. He is not allowed any visitors until further notice. I will be sure to keep you abreast of the situation."

They exchanged goodbyes and left his office.

Trey's arraignment lasted all of twenty minutes. Trey looked well to DeeDee.

"How do you plead, Mr. Wilson?" the Judge asked Trey.

The lawyer spoke before he could. "Your Honor, my client pleads not guilty by reason of insanity."

"Mr. Steinberg, your client has been before this court, with that same plea. I will allow the plea; however, Mr. Wilson must undergo numerous psychiatric evaluations."

"Understood, your Honor."

"This case will be set aside without prejudice. The date will be set on the court calendar pending the outcome of the evaluations. Court is adjoined." The lawyer then told DeeDee he would be in touch.

DeeDee and Liz left the courtroom and Liz said not a word.

"That's a relief," DeeDee said.

"What's a relief, sis?" asked Liz.

"It's good that he is going to be evaluated again. I really think that he is not right in the head. How can they murder a man that's not sane?"

For fear of coming off insensitive and abrupt, Liz once again remained quiet. But Liz could no longer hold her tongue.

"How can he murder innocent people? Don't get me started sis," Liz told DeeDee.

They days were long, DeeDee still had not seen Trey. Every time Trey called to talk to DeeDee, Liz intercepted. She refused to let Trey talk to his mother. She did not want him upsetting her. She was thankful that Trey wasn't allowed visitors, she hoped he would continue to be violent.

The evaluations were completed, the hearing was set two days away. This hearing was to prove if Trey Allan Wilson was competent to stand trial. Judge Myra Perkins entered the courtroom. Everyone took their seats. Trey was handcuffed and shackled. He was also wearing a protected head covering. There were three psychiatrists present, all of whom had an integral part of his evaluation process. The DA questioned each one extensively, then the defense went forward with questioning.

The questing was complete. Judge Perkins asked the defendant to stand, Trey and his lawyer stood before the Judge.

"Mr. Wilson, it is the order of this court that you stand trial for the murders of said persons." The Judge read each name. "The trial date is set for three months from now, on the fifth day of September 2011. Court is adjoined."

Liz was not surprised, DeeDee was in tears. Her son would be scrutinized in the public's eye and judged by twelve people that don't even know him. DeeDee Janell Wilson remained in denial.

Trey remained an outcast, he didn't follow any rules. He remained in solitary confinement most of the time. He was, however, allowed a rare visit from his mother. Trey really didn't want to see her unless she was dead. He conceded to the visit. DeeDee had grown old and weary, but she was still in denial. She entered the booth in the visiting area, glass between the two of them, only phones to communicate. DeeDee picked up the phone, as did Trey.

He spat at the glass. "Why are you here?" I hate you for what you did to me. If you had only gotten rid of those boys, I would not be here. Go away!" he told his mother. "I never want to see you again."

DeeDee jumped from her chair and ran to the exit. She stood by the door and bawled. Liz was downstairs to comfort her sister.

Liz remained loyal to her sister, but as the time went by, DeeDee did not give up on her son. The trial was fast approaching. In two days, she would sit in a courtroom listening to the gory details of the things the police said her son had done. The pictures were gruesome, DeeDee thought her son could never be so cruel as to cold-bloodedly murder those people on the screen. Was she really so naive as to forget what her son had done to her children, his brothers? He killed his own father. He killed four other innocent victims. DeeDee needed to face the reality that Trey, her son, was a monster. He had no remorse.

The trail lasted for three weeks; the jury of his peers came back with a guilty verdict on all counts. Trey didn't utter a single word. He began to laugh uncontrollably. When the sheriffs led him from the courtroom, he was still laughing. Trey would be sentenced in two weeks. He was a sadistic psychopath. I don't believe in the death penalty, but this is the one exception, Dee thought.

Trey and his lawyer appeared before the judge for sentencing. DeeDee and Liz were in the back of the court. The victim statements were heart-wrenching. The judge asked Trey Allan Wilson to stand, he and his lawyer stood before the judge.

"Mr. Wilson, it is the order of this court that you be put to death by lethal injection for the horrendous crimes that you have committed. May God have mercy on your soul. This court is adjourned."

The judge banged her gavel and left her courtroom.

Trey yelled to her, "I will get you!" The sheriffs escorted him away once again. Trey was escorted to Death Row to await his execution date.

His lawyer filed an appeal. It would be unethical for his attorney to quit, but that's what he wanted to do. He had never in his twenty-three years as an attorney encountered a Trey Allan Wilson, or anyone close to the likes of him. He would soon retire. This was his last case.

Trey sat on death row as if he were at the Ritz, he had no remorse about what he had done. He was planning his third escape, only this time he had a foolproof plan.

DeeDee knew that she was in poor health, she pinned over her son, still refusing to accept that he wasn't in his right mind. She and her sister, Liz, never talked about him anymore, it would only start an argument. Trey had made it very clear that he wanted nothing to do with his mother or his aunt. They were both dead to him. If he ever got out again, he was going to make sure that they were dead. Trey had an evil mind, he didn't want to change.

Attorney Steinberg visited the prison twice per month, always on a Tuesday. He had filed an appeal; his first appeal had been denied. His second appeal was coming up soon. The attorney thought that might be a denial as well. He really wanted to pass this case on to his partner so that he could throw in the towel. He didn't have the heart. He wanted Trey to fire him, but that didn't happen. Trey had been on death row for three years; no execution date had been set. He always told the other inmates on the block that he wasn't going to die. He told them he was going to be granted and appeal and his sentence would be overturned.

They all laughed at him. Next cell to his was a serial killer as well. He had been on death row for thirteen years. His name was John Michael, he had been convicted of sixteen counts of murder, his execution date was in two weeks. John Michael's execution had been stayed twice. Trey told John Michael not to concern himself with it because he was going to get another stay. Trey was delusional. Trey was sick in the mind. Mental, everybody knew it but him. And his mother refused to accept that fact. Two weeks went by, Trey's attorney went by the prison, to tell Trey that his last appeal had been exhausted. There were no more appeals and the next step for the process was to set an execution date. Trey spat at the glass between the two men. Trey told his lawyer that he was fired, but little did he know, that was what Attorney Steinberg had been waiting for all along. Steinberg stood up, thanked Mr. Wilson, and walked away. Trey began to bang on the glass with his fist, "Come back here, you call yourself a lawyer, I am here because of you!" It all fell entirely on deaf ears. Attorney Steinberg had made his last and final walk down those halls. He breathed a sigh of relief as he walked to his car, never looking back.

Trey was taken out to the yard once a day. He told himself, "Self, you must find a way to break down these walls and get back to the streets." He didn't mean break down the walls literally, or did he? He saw nothing but wire and steel all around him, there was no way possible he could break out. His breakout days were over. His killing sprees were over, he was doomed. His fate was death. Even if he wasn't put to death, he would die behind those bars. Trey Allan Wilson would never walk the streets has a free man, nor should he.

One day, Trey received a visit from CVAC, Crime Victims Advocacy Council, Charles Northrop read about his case through the council, he needed to meet him. Because of his age, they thought there may be a chance to get him life in prison rather than the death penalty. As Trey listened to Mr. Northrop, his ears perked up. He was very interested in all he had to say.

"So, can you get me out of here?" Trey asked him.

"I am afraid that may not be possible. We start with trying to get you off death row before your execution date. Then, if we are successful, we will continue our quest to get you a lighter sentence with parole. It can be a long and tedious process. First, we must get your permission to go forth."

"You have my permission to go forth, do whatever you need to do to get me out of this place."

"I will be in touch, Mr. Wilson." Mr. Northrop left.

Trey yelled down the hall, "Hey, nut cases! I got somebody working to get me out of this dump. Told you, I wasn't going to die in here." Trey was delusional, Trey Allan Wilson was totally insane. No if, ands, or buts about it. He didn't hear very much of what was just said to him.

DeeDee was feeling much better these days, she had gotten some of her strength back. Her doctor had her on daily vitamins and she was given a B-12 shot once a month. She and Liz were supporting each other, they did everything together, including a daily walk. The house had been just the two of them for a while now, so DeeDee asked her sister what she thought of renting the basement out. It was a small apartment. It hadn't been lived on since Carmen.

Liz thought that was a great idea, plus it would be more company for us. Liz told DeeDee that she would call one of the apartment rental agencies, because they would do the screening for us.

"You know, DeeDee, we are getting up in age, we can't have just anyone living with us."

"You are so right, sis."

"Okay, then it is settled, I will get on it tomorrow," Liz told her.

Trey was in his own world, whistling and singing, just carrying on in his tiny cell. His roomies always asked him what he had to be so happy about. You are on death row man, and you are going to die. Trey had gotten his execution date; however, he was not phased in the least.

"Not going to happen!" he yelled back to those who thought the brother was nuts.

They were right! He was scheduled to be executed in one month. There was still time. Northrop and his peeps were working on getting him out.

Like what was stated many times before, Trey Allan Wilson is not right in the brain.

DeeDee had been notified of her son's execution date. They needed to know if she wanted to attend.

"I will get back to you on that," DeeDee said to the clerk. "I will discuss it with my family and let you know." She was told that if she decided to attend, she was allowed to bring one person for support.

Mr. Northrop had been in contact with DeeDee every step of the way, there had been several attempts to get Trey's case reopened, but to no avail. However, they were dedicated to keep trying until the twelfth hour. That being until his time had run out. A stay would also be requested.

DeeDee talked to her sister about the possibility of watching her son be put to death. She had resigned herself to the fact that it was going to happen. Liz let her sister know that if she didn't want him to be alone, then she would go with her.

The two ladies, sisters, had managed to find a roommate. It was an older man, who was widowed, he sold his house a year ago after his wife passed. He had been searching for a nice roommate, but he didn't like any of them that had been sent his way by the agency. When he heard of the two sisters that were close to his age, he decided to meet with them. His name was Evert Parsons. He met with the sisters at the agency, and he was quite impressed. The three chatted for over an hour. It was a fit. He moved in a week later.

Trey was about to have his last meal of fried chicken, corn, and mashed potatoes. That was his favorite meal when he was younger. His mother made it for him and his dad on special occasions. He was allowed to see his mother if he wanted to. Trey had finally come to the realization that he was going to die by lethal injection, and there was nothing anyone could do. Trey wasn't a prayer, but he felt that he needed to ask God for forgiveness. He prayed as best he knew how. His mother prayed all the time. He was sure she had been praying for her son all the years that had passed.

DeeDee entered the room, a small visiting room. The sheriff brought Trey in handcuffs and shackles. When he saw her, he called out her name, "Mommy!"

She hadn't heard that in years. Now it was the last time she would hear her baby call her anything. DeeDee went over to her son and hugged him tight, they both cried.

"I am so sorry, mother, for all that I have put you through. Please forgive me," he cried to his mother.

"I forgave you long ago, and I have never stopped loving you," she told her son. "I need for you to ask God for forgiveness."

"Yes, mother I have done that, and I am ready to have my misery ended."

"I will be sitting in the front row with your Auntie Liz. Just keep your eyes on me."

It was time for Trey to be taken to the execution chamber. DeeDee held on so tight, the sheriff had to pull them apart. She gave him a kiss on his cheek just as she had always done. She saw her son alive for the last time.

The execution chamber was cold, Trey thought to himself. They strapped him down, so many straps, he thought. They stuck the fluid into the needle, he had tubes in both arms. I remember this, just like when I was in the hospital a long time ago. It was literally a lifetime ago. All the times that had escaped him over the years had returned. He was thinking good thoughts. The curtains were opened, and he saw his mother and his auntie sitting in the front row. He locked eyes on his mother and never took them off her. He mouthed I love you and she returned to the same to him. The warden gave the nod after checking the clock. Trey closed his eyes, let out a cough, and he was gone. He was pronounced dead at 7:22 p.m.

DeeDee cried in her sister's arms, they cried together. Upon leaving the prison, they proceeded to the hearse, they stood until his body was loaded. *Tomorrow she will make the final arrangements. I hope this is the last one of my family members I must lay to rest.* She was hoping that she would pass before her sister.

Trey was laid to rest in all white, just as his brothers and his father. She buried him in the family plot. There were two plots left, one for her and one for her sister. DeeDee placed flowers on all her loved one's graves and went home to rest. It was over.

Thank you Father God for all of YOUR blessings.

www.ingramcontent.com/pod-product-compliance
Lightning Source LLC
LaVergne TN
LVHW091556060526
838200LV00036B/867